all-time great classics

KING ARTHUR
& THE KNIGHTS OF
The Round Table
(A masterpiece of Thomas Malory)

MANOJ PUBLICATIONS

Publishers :

MANOJ PUBLICATIONS

761, Main Road, Burari, Delhi-110084 (INDIA)

Mobile : 09999476076, 09868112194
08178823569, 08178854810

E-mail : info@manojpublications.com

For online shopping visit our website :
www.sawanonlinebookstore.com

From the Publisher's Desk

In this age of competition, none has the time to go through long novels which seem to have no endings. Maybe these kinds of novels were written during the time when people led leisurely life. They had plenty of time at their disposal. Reading good literary work on weekend was the main source of entertainment. Now the time has entirely changed. Readers search for short, excellent literary works which are comprised of well-designed illustrations. These illustrations clear their themes at very first glance. As a reader flips through the pages of an illustrated novel, each chapter unfolds in a very easy and interesting style.

Keeping this modern approach in mind, we have brought out this novel in a very novel way. Easy-to-understand language accompanied by life-like illustrations has added four-fold beauty to the novel. At the end of the novel, questions based on each and every chapter have been given to test the mental faculty of the reader.

All these outstanding features incorporated in this novel have made it suitable for young and old alike. Undoubtedly, it is ideal for classrooms, library and personal collection too.

About the Author

Thomas Malory was born in the year 1430. He was an Englishman. At the time of his birth, England was passing through a phase of civil wars and strife. This had a great impact on the mind of young Malory.

As he grew up, he became violent and obstinate. His father wanted him to be a literary figure but fate had something else in store for young Malory.

At an adolescent age, he joined the army, much against the wish of his father. There in the army, he served under the great Richard Beauchamp, Earl of Warwick and a few others, who moulded him into a great personality.

With the passage of time Malory gave up his job in the army and entered the world of violence. For his nefarious deeds he was arrested and put behind bars. He spent his several years in prison. During that period, the literary mind in him developed and he penned down the wonderful novel–*King Arthur and the Knight of the Round Table*. The novel is about the exploits of the great Arthur in the fifteenth century.

But Thomas Malory did not live long to see his book published. He breathed his last in Newgate Prison on 14 March 1471. He lived for only 41 years. In such a short period, he earned himself name and fame by virtue of his writing the book. That is why it is said– The pen is mightier than the sword. His book was published fourteen years after his death by the famous printer, William Caxton.

Contents

Merlin

King Arthur

Queen Guinevere

Lancelot

Arthur is Crowned King

In olden days, Britain was not a powerful country. It had been divided into small kingdoms. These kingdoms were ruled over by kings. The name of one such king was Uther. He was a benevolent, truthful and justice-loving king. The name of his wife was Igraine. Both the King and the Queen were spending their days peacefully. They were very loyal to their subjects. The subjects, in turn, obeyed their every order. Those were the days when the kings kept themselves busy fighting amongst themselves. Each one of them wanted to show his supremacy over the other.

Time passed by. Queen Igraine gave birth to a baby-boy. The baby-boy was named Arthur. There was atmosphere of happiness in and around the palace. Arthur had a pleasant face. His hair was golden and eyes were big and blue. In all, he was a fair-complexioned baby who was strong too. Both King Uther and Queen Igraine were on cloud nine. Their ecstasy knew no bounds. Arthur was bubbly and had rosy lips. One day, a magician by the name Merlin came to the palace of King Uther. Arthur was by then three days old. With both palms joined in utter reverence he uttered, "Your Highness! I am magician Merlin. I have come here on purpose. If your Majesty permits me, I shall speak my mind."

Hearing of the words of the magician King Uther said to him, "O Magician! Say whatever you want to Utter. Don't fear anybody here. You are free to express yourself without any hesitation."

Magician Merlin uttered thus, "Your Highness! Baby Arthur has become three days old. But I wonder this palace is not fit for him to live in. He has to be raised in the house of one of your brave knights. Only then will he be able to become a brave king."

Hearing of the words of Merlin King Uther was very much surprised. He asked the magician in wonder, "But whom can I trust? I don't see anybody is capable of bringing up my baby-boy like his own son."

The magician paused a little bit and then uttered, "Your Majesty! I have a name in my mind. I think he will be capable of raising your baby to your fullest satisfaction." The King asked him in amazement, "O dear! Tell me who that knight is. I shall do as you tell me as it is the question of the safety of my baby."

Magician Merlin thus uttered, "None other than Sir Ector! He is faithful and loyal. Moreover, he is your true friend. Without any hesitation you can hand over your baby to him. He is very much capable in every respect."

The King observed, "So be it! I act upon your advice. If you so wish, I have no problem as I have faith in you." Saying so he handed the baby across to Magician Merlin.

King Uther was very much aware of the fact that he would not be there in the world to see his son, Arthur, ride his first horse or brandish his first sword. He thought he had better hand over his son to his faithful knight who was quite young and energetic. The knight was in the prime of his youth. He could train child Arthur better in all war tactics.

Magician Merlin having wrapped the baby in his cloak slipped away from the palace under the blanket of darkness. None could notice him while he was leaving the palace.

From there, Merlin straightaway reached the house of Sir Ector. Giving him the baby he said to Sir Ector, "Here is the baby-boy of King Uther and his Queen Igraine. Raise him as your own son and train him efficiently in all the disciplines of warfare."

Sir Ector accepted the baby-boy gladly and uttered, "As you wish, Sir. This baby-boy will be brought up very much to your wish. I shall leave no stone unturned in raising this baby to my fullest capacity and capability. Rest assured the baby will earn name and fame when he grows up."

After handing over the baby to Sir Ector Merlin returned to the palace of King Uther. He started living there. After a few days, King Uther fell seriously ill. The physician who attended upon him said to the Queen, "Dear lady! His living days are numbered. He won't live more than a week."

Hearing of the words of the physician Merlin approached the King and said, "Your Highness! It is high time you should call all your knights, barons and great men and declare that the heir-apparent of this kingdom would be none other than your son, Arthur. Act quickly, otherwise your son will be in distress."

King Uther at once ordered all the knights and barons to gather around him. Then the King declared, "My end is nearing. After my death my son Arthur would be the next king without any opposition."

The knights and barons began to fight among themselves for the crown.

10

Saying these words the King breathed his last. Now the barons and the knights were not ready to accept child Arthur as their new king. Each of them wanted to become the next king of Britain.

A pall of gloom descended upon the palace. But the knights and the barons had no pity for the death of their king. They began to fight among themselves for the crown. In the absence of a new king tyranny and anarchy prevailed over the kingdom. None obeyed the law of the land. There was atmosphere of chaos and confusion all around. With every passing day things went from bad to worse. Fifteen years went by in such fashion. The Britons were passing through a bad phase of life. There were sorrow and trouble for them. In the house of Sir Ector child Arthur by now had attained manhood. But he was unaware of the origin of his birth. Under the able leadership and guidance of Sir Ector Arthur had become a highly skilled warrior.

Sensing the opportune time the wise old Merlin said to himself, 'It is the appropriate time to bring Arthur to the palace. Thinking so he went over to the Archbishop (head of church) and uttered, "Sir! Please call all the barons and the knights here, and declare that Arthur would be their next King." The Archbishop did as he was told. All the knights and the barons gathered together outside the church. The Archbishop called them inside and spoke to them. Thereafter, each of them left the church one by one. When all of them reached outside, they saw in front of the door a marble stone. It had a steel anvil upon it. A naked sword was there in the anvil. The hilt of the sword carried some writing in gold letters. The writing read thus—

"Attention! In order to be the rightful king of Britain one has to pull out the sword from this stone."

Each of the knights tried his level best but all in vain. None could pull out the sword. The Archbishop was seeing all this. He was very much pleased in his heart of hearts. He knew that only Arthur would be able to perform this spectacular feat. He uttered in a low voice, "He has not come as yet. Had he been here the situation would have been different."

After some time he turned to the knights and the barons, and said to them, "Dear! All of you should stay in London and joust (*to fight on horseback using a lance in order to try to knock the other warrior off his horse*). Make it a tournament so that you may stay together. Mind it no person should be stopped from pulling out the sword."

Acting upon the advice of the Archbishop the knights conducted a great joust in London. The knights of other kingdom too were invited to take part in the contest. The names of the invitation reached Sir Ector as well. He along with his own son, Sir Kay, and Arthur went to take part in the competition. Both Sir Kay and Arthur were in their teens and excited to take part in the joust. While they were on their way to the joust-site, Sir Kay all of a sudden exclaimed, "Oh no! I have forgotten my sword at the lodgings."

After a while, he said do Arthur, "Dear brother, if you don't mind, would you go back and bring my sword? I can't proceed without my sword."

Arthur as obedient he was, readily accepted to ride back and fetch his brother's sword. He at once turned back and rode off towards the lodgings. To his utter surprise, there was none in the lodgings. All the doors were locked. Everyone had gone to watch the tournament.

Arthur said to himself, 'What should I do now? Should I return without the sword or should I wait here for somebody to come?' An idea struck to his mind. He thought, 'I can give my sword to Sir Kay. He needs it more than I.' Thinking so he rode back as hurriedly as he could. The horse was running with the speed of the wind. As the horse rode past the churchyard, Arthur all of a sudden pulled the reins of his horse. The horse stopped at once. He dismounted from his horse and went over to the steel anvil wherein there was a naked sword. Seeing the sword Arthur exclaimed with surprise, 'Wow! What a beautiful mighty sword! I had better pull it out and give it to Sir Kay. He will be very delighted to possess it.'

Thinking so he grabbed the mighty handle of the sword with both his hands and pulled it out with all his might. The sword came out without much difficulty. After getting the sword Arthur felt elated. He jumped onto his horse and rode off towards the joust-site. After reaching Sir Kay he handed over the sword to Sir Kay who was on cloud nine. Sir Kay at once recognized the sword and turned to his father, "Dear Father! Now I have this sword. It means I am the new ruler of Britain."

Sir Ector was utterly surprised seeing the sword there in the hand of Sir Kay. He asked, "Dear Son! But how have you got this sword? If I am not mistaken, this must be the handiwork of Arthur."

Sir Kay observed, "Yes father, you are very much right. Arthur has given me this sword just now."

Sir Ector turned to Arthur and asked, "Dear son! How did you get it?"

Arthur without any hesitation replied, "Dear father, while I was returning past the churchyard, I saw this sword in the steel anvil. So, I pulled it out to be given it to my brother, Sir Kay." Hearing of the words of Arthur Sir Ector was beside himself with joy. He said to Sir Kay, "Dear, your brother Arthur is the real king of this land. We both should kneel down before him."

Saying these words both Sir Ector and Sir Kay bowed in front of Arthur. They were all praise for their new King. Seeing his brother and father kneeling down before him Arthur was overwhelmed with emotion. He uttered, "O dear father and brother! You are my loved ones. Why do you bow in front of me? It hurts me a lot. Please don't do this."

Hearing of the words of Arthur Sir Ector realized that it was the opportune time for him to tell Arthur the real story of his birth. Gathering courage he observed, "Dear Arthur, you are not my real son. I adopted you long time ago. Your father was King Uther and your mother was Queen Igraine." Saying these words Sir Ector told him the entire story. Having known about his real parents Arthur felt disappointed and dejected. He was crestfallen. He fell into an abyss of despair. He started weeping inconsolably. Sir Ector patted his back out of affection and said, "Be a god lad; don't weep over your past. Try to live in the present, for tomorrow comes in the form of present. Do promise me that you would rule over your subjects in an efficient manner. You would prove yourself to be an able administrator."

Arthur made a promise to Sir Ector that he would leave no stone unturned in proving himself an able ruler and administrator.

Thereafter, all of them went over to the Archbishop who called all the knights and the barons. When all of them gathered together in the churchyard, the

Archbishop said to them, "Listen carefully. Your next king would be Arthur."

Hearing of the words of the Archbishop all the knights and the barons flew into a rage. Just then, Merlin the magician appeared there and said to Arthur, "Dear son, put the sword back into the steel anvil." Arthur did as he was told.

The knights and the barons felt surprised and shocked. They all asked in one voice, "What does it mean? Does it convey that Arthur would be the king?" Merlin at once pointed to some words written at the bottom of the stone. Then he addressed the gathering, "Let me tell you very clearly what is written on the stone. Would all of you like to lend your ears to me? I read out in a loud voice—whosoever pulls out the sword from the steel anvil shall be the rightful heir to the throne of Britain."

The knights said to Merlin, "It is a child's play to pull out the sword from this stone. Let us try once again."

Saying so all the knights and the barons one by one tried once again. But all their efforts proved an exercise in futility. On the other hand, Arthur once again pulled out the sword from the steel anvil with great ease. Merlin felt pleased. He said to the assembly of the knights and the barons, "Look this is the quality of true king. You must all be very anxious to know who this Arthur is. Well, Arthur is the son of King Uther and his Queen Igraine. When Arthur was born, I discovered by foresight that somebody had plotted inside the palace to put an end to him."

"As a true loyal friend of King Uther, I suggested to him to shift child Arthur somewhere else. The King

"*No Merlin, every Tom, Dick and Harry can't be our King*," *said King Lot of Orkney.*

acted upon my sound advice and allowed me to take the child away from the palace to the house of Sir Ector, King's long-term friend. There, Sir Ector raised the child as his own son. This is how I was able to save child Arthur. Now, he has fulfilled the condition; he is very much capable of being crowned the next king of Britain."

But the knights and the barons were bent upon having their say. They didn't see eye to eye with Merlin. One of the old and powerful knights observed, "O Merlin, how can we accept an unknown youth to be our next king? How can you say that the blood of King Uther is running through his veins. Do you have any proof to validate your statement?"

Then, King Lot of Orkney came forward and said angrily, "No Merlin, every Tom, Dick and Harry can't be our king. Arthur seems to be a street urchin. How can he rule over us?"

Then came forward King Mark of Cornwall. He too uttered in an angry tone, "What nonsense this is! You are making a mockery of courageous people like us. Your declaration seems to be a cock-and-bull story. It is a white lie which has no legs to stand upon."

But Merlin was more than a watch for all of them. He observed, "Keep cool, O knights and barons. It is no deceit. I am speaking the truth, and only truth. Each and every word of my story is true. There is not an iota of falsehood in it. Well, feast days are approaching. The same test of grit and courage can be had on the next three feast days."

"If only Arthur is successful in pulling out the sword he shall be the rightful king of Britain." The knights and the barons agreed to the suggestion of Merlin. Very soon, the feast of Candlemas came. Each and every knight and baron was put through the test of grit. But all of them failed in their job. Only Arthur succeeded in pulling out the sword. Next, there came Easter feast. The same thing happened their. Only Arthur did his job in great fashion. All the knights and the barons tried level best but to no purpose. They couldn't even budge the sword an inch from its position. The third and final test was to take place on the feast of Pentecost. A large crowd gathered outside the church. With great elan and ease Arthur pulled out the sword in one jerk and whirled it round his head. The croud was on cloud nine. They shouted gleefully, "Long live our king Arthur! May God grant him all the riches of the world! May he conquer the entire world!"

Once again it was the victory of Arthur. The knights and the barons hung their heads in shame. They felt ashamed of their misdeed. They too accepted Arthur as their new king. They lay prostrate at the feet of Arthur and begged their forgiveness for doubting his power. Arthur patted their backs and hugged them to his bosom. Thereafter, he addressed the gathering, "O dear friends! I Arthur, son of King Uther and Queen Igraine, take pledge today that I shall be over loyal to my land. I shall try my level best to drive out the enemies from our land and establish the reign of truthfulness and nobility."

Thereafter, Arthur was taken inside the church where he was crowned the new king of Britain.

The Fellowship of Knights

Arthur had become King Arthur. He had pledged to bring place and honour to the kingdom. Arthur's path was beset with several obstacles. After the death of Uther, the Saxon pirates had raised their ugly heads and were becoming stronger and stronger. They were very cruel. They started raiding the coastal cities and plundered them completely. They had no fear of anybody. Their ships started sailing up the rivers deep in the countryside. Added to this they came over there to settle down, constructing their own dwellings and making them like fortresses. They were very crafty people.

On the other hand in the kingdom of King Arthur many of the knights and the barons were not happy with Arthur being the king. They hated him very much. Somehow, they wanted to dethrone their new king. So, they joined together and discussed this grave issue deeply. At last, they planned to usurp the throne by hook or by crook. After consulting his loyal ministers and other prominent associates King Arthur decided to shift his court to the fortress town of Camelot. This town had been built by the Romans. From there, it was quite easy for King Arthur to do administrative functions. Riding on straight and plain Roman roads it was two days march to the new Saxon settlements. Moreover, these Roman roads also led to the lands and the castles of the rebel lords. King Arthur had stationed himself there for quite some time. One day, a spy reached king Arthur and informed him thus, "Your Majesty! The Saxons are planning to wage war on us. We are being attacked from all sides. Do act quickly or it will be late."

King Arthur grew worried having listened to the words of the spy. But he was not cowardly. He was a brave man. He contacted King Leodegrance who ruled over the kingdom of Cameliard. King Leodegrance was a best friend of late King Uther. It so happened that the rebel army was marching through the kingdom of Cameliard. So, King Leodegrance pleaded King Arthur to hold off the rebels. Though his army was small yet he was determined. Now King Arthur was a little bit relieved. But he had a lot of work to do. He approached Sir Bedivere and asked him to ride south and attack the Saxons. Thereafter, he asked Sir Kay and Magician Merlin to stay behind and stand guard at Camelot. After entrusting the task to them King Arthur himself at the head of a large army marched towards the kingdom of Cameliard.

King Arthur on his white horse was looking majestic. The subjects of Camelot waved and cheered their King. They wished for his long life. After late King Uther, it was King Arthur who had won the hearts of his subjects by his deed and thought. King Arthur along with his large army rode on and on, day in and day out. At the eleventh hour they reached Cameliard where the Saxons had an upper hand over the forces of King Leodegrance. Seeing this King Arthur ordered his army to wage war on the Saxons. A fierce battle ensued between the forces of the Saxons on one side and the combined forces of King Arthur and King Leodegrance. The battle went on till evening. Many a knight on either side fell. As the evening was approaching, King Arthur had a face-to-face encounter with the rebel leader of the Saxons.

Seeing him in front of him King Arthur's blood boiled with rage. He got very much furious. With one single stroke of his sword he did away with the rebel leader. Seeing his leader dead the Saxon forces raised a hue and cry. They started running helter-skelter in order to save their lives. But none could escape from there. At last, all of them surrendered to King Arthur. They laid down their weapons and sought King Arthur's mercy. King Arthur, as benevolent he was, showed mercy to the knights and the barons who had turned against him. The knights and the barons hung their heads in shame. They were all praise for King Arthur. They said to King Arthur, "We all swear in the name of Jesus Christ that we shall be ever loyal to you in the future. None can dare attack you in our presence."

Hearing their words King Arthur was beside himself with joy. Now it was party time. A grand feast was organized in the court of king Leodegrance. All the members wined and dined together throughout the night. King Arthur was pleased on two counts. Firstly, the knights and the barons who had turned against him had come over to his side. Secondly, Sir Bedivere who had gone to the south to stall the advance of the Saxons had defeated them completely. Added to this, he along with his army burnt down their houses and pushed them back into the sea. The celebration went on throughout the night. Everybody present there was under the influence of liquor. King Arthur had proved

Merlin observed, "It is not appropriate, my dear son."

his mettle. In the feast, the daughter of King Leodegrance made her presence felt. King Arthur fell in love with her. It was love at first sight. He had never seen before such a beautiful lass. She too found King Arthur to be brave and intelligent.

As soon as King Arthur returned to his kingdom after the mission was over, he at once sent for Merlin. When Merlin presented himself in front of King Arthur, the latter observed, "Dear Merlin you have been serving us for quite a long time. You are the most loyal person I have in my kingdom. Right now, I am entrusting you with an important task. Do it carefully. Go to the kingdom of king Leodegrance and seek his permission so that I may marry his beautiful daughter."

Hearing the words Merlin observed, "Dear son! It is not appropriate. This marriage won't bring you any reward. If I am not mistaken, it will bring in misery only. So, don't go in for this marriage."

But King Arthur was bent upon marrying the daughter of King Leodegrance. Merlin had no alternative but to go to King Leodegrance.

Merlin was welcomed with great warmth. King Leodegrance himself received him with great respect. After the formal refreshment Merlin told king Leodegrance the purpose of his visit.

Hearing the words of Merlin the King was on cloud nine. He was beside himself with joy. He said to Merlin, "What a piece of happy news you have brought! Long live King Arthur! I feel relaxed and relieved that the worthy king of Camelot is going to marry my only daughter Guinevere."

"Will your daughter marry our king?" asked Merlin in surprise. King Leodegrance observed, "Yes, why not.

She can't find a match better than King Arthur. Moreover, she never refuses to do what I say to her. Rest assured, she will marry the King without any doubt."

Merlin returned to Camelot the same day and delivered the happy news to King Arthur. Hearing the happy news king Arthur's joy knew no bounds. He patted the back of Merlin and hugged him to his bosom. As per the then tradition, the daughter of King Leodegrance left Cameliard for Camelot with her attendants. She was dressed in her best finery. She was wearing a lot of jewellery. She was looking really stunning. The subjects of Camelot were very excited to see a glimpse of their new queen. A lot of people gathered on either side of the road. As the queen entered the outskirts of Camelot, the subjects began to shout loudly, "Long live the Queen! Cheers to our Queen!"

Guinevere stayed at the palace of King Arthur. A priest was called to fix the date of the marriage. After all done, the city was decorated tastefully with the flowers and the branches of green trees. The great church was repainted from inside as well from outside. It was decorated with white and pink flowers. Soon, the day of wedding arrived. The entire city of Camelot was in high spirit. A saintly old priest was called in to solemnize the ceremony. After much fanfare and happiness the ceremony came to an end. The people who had gathered outside the church cheered their king and new queen. They raised slogans in their appreciation. King Arthur had received a lot of gifts from the neighbouring kings. King Leodegrance, father of the bride, gave him the gifts of gold and silver. Among the gifts was an enormous round table. It has been presented to him by late king Uther. One of the main features of this round table was that a hundred and fifty knights could sit around it at one time. Several knights were also sent in his service.

These knights had pledged to serve King Arthur. Days passed by followed by weeks and months. One morning, King Arthur was sitting at the round table. He looked at the table very carefully. He felt very elated when he realized that the table was really a special gift from his father-in-law. Since it was round, none of the knights could sit at a place higher than any other. This way, no one would think himself to be more superior to the other. It had other aspect as well. Nobody would be thought more in the King's favour. Sitting at the round table all the knights would be treated as equals. Such was the quality of the round table. King Arthur sent for his prominent and loyal knights. When they all appeared there, he said to them, "Hello friends, how are you? I have called all of you to me on purpose. Let us see how many of you are determined to serve me till their last breath. He who serves me is required to take an oath of Fellowship– The Fellowship of the Round Table. This is no ordinary round table."

"The seats on the round table are meant for the brave, wise and worthy knights who are ready to give up their all for the honour and integrity of their country. Those who take an oath here are required to dedicate their entire life to the honour of their country. They are to promise today that they will establish the reign of nobility, dedicate their life to the service of God and protect the downtrodden, the weak and the helpless."

Hearing the words of King Arthur all the knights and the barons looked at one another. Sir Ector came

Merlin observed, "Kind attention,
all noble knights and barons."

forward and took the oath without any hesitation. He was the first knight to do so. While taking an oath he raised his glittering sword.

The moment he did so, the clouds thundered threateningly outside. There was a flash of lightning across the clouds. All of a sudden, the lights in the hall went out. The hall was completely plunged into utter darkness. After a minute or so, the lights came back. King Arthur noticed that there was a knight's name written on every seat of the table. It was really very amazing. What amazed king Arthur sore was that there was a seat whereupon no name was written. Some words were written there which read as follows—'None but the world's truest knight deserves this seat.'

King Arthur could not figure out anything. He asked his wise knights and barons what it meant. But none gave a satisfactory response. Now, King Arthur turned to Merlin and asked in wonder, "Sir! Can you tell us what these words written on the seat mean? This thing is troubling me. Please say something about it."

Merlin the magician thought for a while. Then he observed, "Kind attention, all noble knights and barons. Please listen to me carefully because what I am going to tell you all, is something very serious. This seat over there is known by the name—Seat Perilous. It holds a significant position. The seat is meant for the knight, who never did anything wrong or shall do nothing wrong in the future as well. One important point is there to note carefully. If a wicket knight happens to sit on the seat, he will surely die. So, keep in mind the points that I have told you all. To my mind, such knight hasn't come as yet. But he is sure to reach here at an opportune time. I firmly believe in this supposition."

Hearing the words of Merlin all the knights and the barons started looking sideways. None of the knights and the barons present there was capable of possessing the seat. After a while, Merlin took out a cloth-piece of gold silk from his pocket and placed it gently over Seat Perilous. He did so just to honour the knight who had yet to come to possess the seat.

Thereafter, all the knights and the barons–Sir Ector, Sir Kay, Sir Bedivere, Sir Owen, Sir Garvaine, Sir Bors, Sir Geraint, Sir Balin, to name a few–stepped forward to possess their respective seats. Before sitting on his seat, each of the knights and the barons took out his sword from the sheath and brandished it in the air. By doing so they showed their courage and loyalty to the kingdom. Each of them took the oath of fellowship and sat on the seat which had his name. As the round table was quite big in size, there remained several empty seats.

When everyone took his seat comfortably, King Arthur addressed them thus, "My dear friends, always remember–united we stand, divided we fall. Never quarrel among themselves. In the future, we shall meet on the three feast days on which I pulled out the sword from the steel anvil. During the three days, each of us will relate his adventure he has had and discuss something new he plans to undertake. I hope and am more than sure that these empty seats over there will be duly filled by brave and chivalric warriors in the time to come. Let the fame of the fellowship of the knights of the Round Table spread far and wide."

❑

Arthur Befriends Sir Pellinore

Now Arthur had become the new king of Britain. Every other day, he would travel all over the country in order to know more about his people. He would land a helping hand to the needy, the unfortunate, the downtrodden and the helpless. Everybody in his kingdom was happy and satisfied. On one such travel, he lost his way and reached a dense forest. Evening was approaching. He thought, 'What should I do now? It is stark dark. It is quite impossible to trace the path that leads to my palace.' Lost in such thoughts, he happened to see a castle which was at a stone's throw from him. The castle was quite big and beautiful. King Arthur had never seen such a huge castle before in his life. He was very much surprised to see the castle there in the dense forest.

King Arthur could not help going near to the castle. No sooner did he reach the gate of the castle than the great door opened. He stood there motionless. Queen Annoure who was a magician appeared there and welcomed the King saying, "Hello dear, how do you do? Why don't you stay in my castle tonight? Evening has approached and the path is beset with wild beasts. Moreover, you must be very hungry. You need to have some food and a bed to sleep on. What do you say?"

The King was taken in by the oily tongue of Queen

Annoure who had plotted an evil game against the King. Holding the hand of the Queen the king walked into the castle with great élan. After he had taken his diner the Queen called out to her personal maid and said, "Take the King to his plush bedroom. An attendant will attend to him throughout the night."

The maid took the king to his bedroom and went away. Seeing the room the king was amazed at its beauty. He had never such kind of architecture inside the room. He slept on a mattress which as soft as velvet. Soon he fell fast asleep. Next morning the Queen came over to him and said, "Hello dear! How was the night? Did you feel any problem? Did you spend the night peacefully?"

Hearing the words of the Queen the King observed, "Yes dear lady. It is all because of you. I slept soundly all through the night. The attendant attended on me nicely. It is really kind of you to have received your guest with such warmth."

After serving breakfast to the King Queen Annoure said to him, "Dear, let me show you my castle. I think it is the biggest and most beautiful castle in the entire kingdom. Apart from this, I possess a large quantity of gold and jewels in my trunk. I think it is much more than anybody has." Hearing the words of the Queen King Arthur was much impressed. He admired the beauty of the castle and of the Queen as well. Thereafter, The Queen took him from one room to another. Each room was more beautiful and richer than the previous one. The king felt amazed at seeing such wealth.

After showing all the rooms to the king the Queen led him to the top of the castle from there one could see a glimpse of the entire kingdom. Reaching there the Queen said to the King, "Look dear, over there are beautiful gardens, lawns and nurseries. There are green fields and orchards where the trees are laden with delicious, juicy fruits. As far as your eyes can reach, all these territories are mine. I have amassed huge wealth over the years."

"All these gardens, green fields sprawling over a large tract of land, orchards and what not belong to me. I kindly request you to stay here with me and be the king of them all. All will respect and obey you. None will go against your wish. You will be the supreme ruler of all the region here."

But King Arthur was not at all interested in staying there. He most humbly said to the Queen, "O fair lady! I respect your good wish and sincerity. But it is next to impossible for me to stay here. Who will care for my subjects over there in Britain? No, I can't part from my citizens who are like children to me."

Hearing the words of the king the Queen flew in rage. She was red with anger. She at once went mad like a stray bull. She yelled at the king and observed, "No, never. You can't get away from here. How dare you refuse my command? I see how you escape from here. For your kind information, the door of the castle has been shut. There are huge walls all around the castle. However hard you may try, you can't get away from here. If you happen to get away from here somehow, you will get killed by my faithful soldiers. So, you had better see eye to eye with me and stay here with me for good. Only then can I spare your life."

But King Arthur was not a man to be feared by such words. He thought for a while and stated, "Who is going

King Arthur raised his sword high
in the air and stamped his feet.

to stop me from going away. You don't know who I am. I am not scared of either you or your magic or your so-called soldiers. I see who stops my way. He who loves his life should not come in front of my way."

Saying these words king Arthur raised his sword high in the air and stamped his feet. Then he hurried out of the castle and out through the front door. All the soldiers of Queen Annoure kept standing there motionless. Not any of them budged an inch from his stand. Seeing all this the Queen got all the more angry and frustrated. Her blood was boiling with rage. She said to herself, 'I must teach King Arthur a bitter lesson. How dare he go against my will?'

After thinking coolly she hit upon a plan. She called out to one of her soldiers and said, 'Go at once to the house of Sir Pellinore. Say to him that an evil knight is bent upon looting my wealth. He has been terrorizing our people for a long time."

The messenger rode off quickly. Queen Annoure wanted to take revenge at any cost. Reaching the house of Sir Pellinore the messenger read out the message to him, "Sir, I am in great distress. An evil knight who lives near by is planning to attack my castle and deprive me of my gold and jewels. Please come to my rescue and do away with this mender."

Sir Pellinore at once stood up from his seat and said to the messenger, "Go and say to your mistress that she need not feel afraid of this trouble-creator. I shall deal with him with a firm hand. Rest assured, I shall do away with him in no time."

The messenger rode back to the castle and delivered the message to the Queen. Hearing the words the Queen was beside herself with happiness. She wanted to lower the esteem of King Arthur by hook or by crook. At the head of a large army Sir Pellinore marched towards the knight who was totally unaware of his approaching there.

Seeing the knight in front of him, Sir Pellinore challenged him to fight against him. Sir Pellinore with a spear in his hand ran towards King Arthur. Then, he hit him hard with the spear. King Arthur was thrown off his horse badly. Getting up quickly king Arthur drew out his sword from his sheath and challenged Sir Pellinore. Now, both the warriors began to fight with their swords. A fierce battle ensued between the two. Both were unmatched. Neither of them was able to overpower the other. They fought fiercely all through afternoon. While fighting a sword duel king Arthur's sword broke into two pieces all of a sudden. Seeing this Sir Pellinore burst out laughing. He yelled at king Arthur and remarked, "O stupid fellow! Even your weapon is not with you. It too is fearing me. Look! How your sword has broken into two pieces! You had better admit your defeat and surrender to me. I promise that I shall spare your life. Act as I tell you, otherwise I shall put you to death."

Hearing the words of Sir Pellinore King Arthur flew into a rage. He was not a fellow to be intimidated by jacket threats. He roared out loudly and uttered, "Look Sir Pellinore! I am not going to lay down my arms in front of you. You can put me to death if you wish so. But I shall fight it out till my last breath. None can say that I am a coward. It has been rightly said cowards die many a time but the brave die once." Saying these words King Arthur leapt forward like a tiger and pulled Sir Pellinore down from his horse. Thereafter he jumped onto him and rained one blow after the other. It all took place in the twinkling of an eye.

Sir Pellinore was taken aback. He had never expected such move from king Arthur. Before he could do anything, it was all over. In full fury, King Arthur tied both the hands of Sir Pellinore at the back. Thus he overpowered him completely. Till now Sir Pellinore was thinking that he had been in face to face with a knight. As King Arthur removed his helmet, Sir Pellinore stood there aghast. His lips fumbled for words. He was on the horns of dilemma. Sir Pellinore lay prostrate at the feet of King Arthur and begged his forgiveness. Tears were rolling down his cheeks. He said to King Arthur, "O great King! I beg your pardon. Shame on me! As a matter of fact, Queen Annoure had ordered me to do away with an evil knight. I am absolutely guiltless. Please forgive me for this grave sin as I was totally unaware of her motive. I was totally unknown that you were there in the garb of a knight."

Saying these words Sir Pellinore began to weep bitterly. King Arthur was, in fact, kind at heart. He knew that Sir Pellinore was not guilty. He was a mere puppet in the hands of the Queen. He raised him up and embraced him to his bosom. He said to Sir Pellinore, "Sir! From today onwards we shall be true friends. Now the time has come to tackle with the Queen jointly. Always remember—united we stand, divided we fall." From that day onwards, both King Arthur and Sir Pellinore became fast friends. Sir Pellinore had promised to help King Arthur in whatever way he would do in future.

After bidding goodbye to Sir Pellinore King Arthur rode back to Camelot. After reaching Camelot, he met

**An arm with a sword in its hand
was coming out of the water.**

Merlin and narrated him the entire incident that took place between him and Sir Pellinore.

After a while, Arthur told Merlin, "Dear, I have broken my sword during my fight against Sir Pellinore. Now I have no sword at all to fight against my enemy. What should I do now? How can I come by a powerful sword?"

After thinking for a few moments Merlin observed, "Fear not, O brave Arthur. You will have a sword which nobody in the entire world has had yet. Follow me without any question."

Hearing the words of Merlin Arthur felt very pleased. He at once rode his horse and followed Merlin who too was on horseback.

After cutting their way through a dense forest, they reached an open place. There, Arthur could see the sky as there were no trees at all. But there was a lake. Merlin told Arthur, "Dear Son! Go near the lake and look into its water. You will get a magic sword."

As directed by Merlin Arthur went near the lake and looked into its water. When he saw inside, it amazed him completely. By and by, an arm with a sword in its hand was coming out of the water. Arthur failed to understand it. He was completely at his wits' end. He could make neither head nor tail of this. He looked at Merlin in bewilderment. Thereupon Merlin explained to him, "Don't get perplexed, dear son. This sword is meant for you. It is called Excalibur, which means—made of steel. It has been specially made for you by the goddess of this lake. Pray to the goddess and appease her. Then, ask her to give you the sword."

With both palms joined in utter reverence Arthur prayed to the goddess with single-pointed devotion. He shut his eyes and uttered, "O Sweet Lady of the lake! I am King Arthur. I have no sword at my disposal. Would you be kind enough to give this sword to me?"

Feeling pleased with the prayer of Arthur the goddess of the lake, appeared in front of him and said, "O dear Arthur, I know you are a brave king. Moreover, you are a noble king who looks after his subjects very well. In your eyes nobody is above the law–poor or rich. This sword is meant for the knight who is very sincere and justice-loving. He who makes no distinction on grounds of caste, colour and creed is a true king. Remember, as long as you have this sword, nothing can harm you. But this sword must be employed to establish the reign of equality, not to establish the reign of injustice."

Saying these words the goddess handed over the sword to Arthur who gladly received it. Thereupon, the goddess disappeared in a trice. After gaining the sword both Arthur and Merlin rowed across to reach the old barge which was at the side of the lake. All of a sudden, the scabbard of the sword let go of the hand of Arthur and slipped away under the water. The scabbard was embedded with jewels, each costlier than the other. Arthur cried in pain, "Oh no! The scabbard has gone under the water. It is very costly." Saying these words Arthur felt disappointed.

Seeing the miserable condition of Arthur Merlin observed, "Dear Son! Why are you sad and disappointed? The sword which does the work is in your hand. So, why are you fretting so much about the scabbard? Tell me what do you like the most–scabbard or sword?"

Without losing a minute Arthur replied, "Dear, undoubtedly it is sword. Now I possess it. Nobody can harm me in any way as long as I have it."

Arthur's Scabbard is Lost

King Uther, Arthur's father had a step-sister. Her name was Morgan le Fay. She hated Arthur very much. She wanted to do away with him by hook or by crook. The reason for her ill-will towards Arthur was that she wanted her son Mordred to sit on the throne of Britain. But there was one obstacle between the throne and her son. It was none other than Arthur. Day in, day out, she kept on thinking as how to get rid of Arthur. Morgan le Fay was a great magician. She possessed great magical powers as superb as those of Merlin.

Inwardly, she had strong resentment against Arthur, but outwardly, she loved Arthur very much. She never showed her ill-will towards him. On the other hand, Arthur too never had any doubt as regards her love for him. But Merlin was quite awake to her nature. He always remained on guard. He was Arthur's shadow. Wherever Arthur visited, Merlin followed him and guided him from time to time. Morgan le Fay pretended to be in the good books of Arthur who loved her like he loved his mother.

One morning, Arthur decided to go hunting. He rode his horse, taking his spear in his hand. Before leaving for the forest he met Morgan le Fay and said to her, "Dear aunt, I am going to the forest to enjoy a pleasure trip. Please take care of this magic sword of mine. Once I get back from the forest, I shall have its from you. Do take care of it. It is quite magical."

There, in the dense forest, Arthur along with his some men went on and on. After a while he lost his way. All his men got separated from him. Soon the evening approached and it was pitching dark. Now Arthur was all alone. But Arthur was a brave knight. All a sudden, he sighted some light at a distance. He rode towards the light. Reaching near the light he found that it was the light of a ship. The ship was ashore. It had cast anchor there for some days. Arthur wanted to get some information, but there was nobody. As the ship was close to the land, Arthur went inside. He reached the first floor of the ship. There he entered a room. He found a table, which was laden with food and drink. Beside the table there was a bed to sleep on. He said to himself, 'This is a good place to take some rest. I can eat and drink here. After sleeping here for the night I shall get off in the morning.' Thinking so Arthur ate to his heart's content. Thereafter, he drank a lot of wine.

After wining and dining he stretched out on the bed lying there. Early tomorrow morning he got up. He had a sound sleep at night. But to his utter dismay, he found that he was not inside the ship. He was in a little room which had only a little window.

Now, Arthur grew worried. He tried to get out of the room but all her efforts proved an exercise in futility. The room was properly locked from outside. Three knights were there in one corner of the room. They too had been locked up like Arthur.

In fact, Arthur had been imprisoned there. It was no ship. But it was the castle of Sir Damas. One of the knights came up to Arthur and said, "O dear, we all have been locked up here. There is no way out from here. Unless and until we fight for Sir Damas, we can't get out however hard we may try."

Just then, some soldiers came up to the cell wherein Arthur and some other knights had been locked up. They unlocked the door of the cell and entered inside. Seeing Arthur and the knights, the soldiers observed thus, "O knights! Our chief Sir Damas has called you all in the hall. Follow us quickly."

Arthur thought for a while and then uttered, "I am not slave to your Sir Damas. Go and tell him that I am not ready to abide by his order. If he is interested in meeting me, he should come over here in my cell."

Seeing the impudence of Arthur the soldiers took out their swords and went ahead to attack Arthur. But the other knights who were standing there intervened and stopped the soldiers from punishing Arthur. They said to the soldiers, "You go and tell Sir Damas that we are coming into the hall."

Hearing the words of the knights the soldier went away. After they had gone away the knights requested Arthur, "Dear, we know you are brave. But the situation demands a little bit submission to Sir Damas. Let us see who Sir Damas is and how courageous he is. Please come along. It will be good for all of us."

Hearing the words of the knights, Arthur thought for a while. Sensing the gravity of the situation Arthur got ready to meet Sir Damas in the hall. Thus Arthur along with all the knights reached the hall where Sir Damas was sitting on a high throne. Seeing Arthur he asked, "Who are you? Where do you come from? Give me your introduction at once."

Arthur with both hands folded observed, "O Sir

Damas! I am Arthur, the king of Britain. I landed here accidentally as I had lost my way."

Then Sir Damas asked, "Tell me whether you will fight for me or not. If you say 'yes', you will be freed from here. In case your reply is in the negative, you are destined to die here in your cell."

Arthur thought coolly and then after some time he uttered, "Well, I can fight for you, but I have a condition. I require these three knights during joust. Only then can I fight for you. After I and these three knights have fought for you, we all shall go back to our respective homes."

Sir Damas was a shrewd knight. He thought for some time and uttered, "Ok, I have no problem. But remember, you and these three knights have to fight for me, come what may."

Just then, a messenger reached the hall of Sir Damas and addressed Sir Damas, "Sir! Here is the sword Excalibur for Arthur. It has been sent by his aunt Morgan le Fay. It is said that it is a magic sword. Whosoever possess it can never be defeated in the war."

Hearing the words of the messenger Sir Damas felt very happy. Equally happy was Arthur who received his magic sword with great pride. Now he was on cloud nine as he had got his powerful sword. Thereupon he said to Sir Damas, "Sir! I am ready for the joust."

Sir Damas painted to his solder and said, "Lead Arthur to the jousting field where he is to fight against another knight." The soldier accompanied by Arthur reached the field. Arthur saw another knight standing there. But his face except his eyes was completely covered. He was not being recognized. Moreover, there was no mark on his shield showing who he was. Arthur was a bit perplexed. But it was not time for thinking over the issue. Soon there ensued a fight between the two. Arthur firmly believed that he possessed a powerful sword in his hand.

The knight made a massive attack on Arthur. But Arthur nullified the attack by lifting his Excalibur. As Arthur's Excalibur hit against the knight's sword, it made no impact. It was unable to bite on the knight's shield. It was no longer sharp and strong. It had lost its sheen and sharpness. Arthur grew worried. He suspected some foul play. He thought, 'Maybe my Excalibur has been changed. This new sword has been made to look like it. There is surely something wrong at the bottom. But what can be done now?' So Arthur kept on fighting without caring for the sword. All of a sudden, Arthur's sword broke into two.

Seeing his broken sword, Arthur was amazed. He could not believe his eyes. He now was dead sure that his Excalibur had been changed and he was fighting with some other sword. The other knight gave out a loud guffaw. He taunted Arthur saying, "I have been told that you are very powerful. Equally powerful is your sword. But alas! The sword of yours is not so powerful. It has landed you in the jaws of death. I can let you go from here unhurt provided you admit that you have lost the fight and don't want to fight further. Moreover, you request me to grant you life."

Hearing the words of the knight Arthur flew into a rage. He shouted at the knight saying, "How dare you say these words to me? Don't you know who I am? I am Arthur, king of Britain." Saying these words Arthur with all his might hit the knight on his hand with his broken sword. The impact was so powerful that the

The moment Arthur touched the sword,
he knew that it was his real Excalibur.

knight lost the grip of his sword. The sword lay flat on the ground. Grabbing the opportunity Arthur at once picked up the knight's sword.

The moment Arthur touched the sword, he knew that it was his real Excalibur. He was now confirmed that some plot had been hatched to kill him. He put the Excalibur on the neck of the knight and threatened him saying, "Speak the truth, O wolf in the sheep's clothing. How have you got this sword? Reveal your identity or I will kill you there and then."

The knight was carrying the sheath or scabbard of the sword. Arthur snatched it too from him. Arthur again uttered, "O knight! If you speak the truth, I shall grant you a new lease of life. In case you tell a lie, you are doomed to die this very moment. The decision is yours. Either be my confidante or get ready to be killed."

The knight after some time observed, "O dear, you know me. I am the knight of the Round Table."

Hearing the words Arthur stood aghast. He asked the knight to reveal his identity properly. Thereupon the knight removed his mark. Now Arthur could see his face. Thus the knight stated, "I am Sir Accolon. I have been sent by your aunt Morgan le Fay." Saying these words he elaborated the entire story. "Thus your aunt told me that you had been taken prisoner by Sir Damas in his castle. She ordered me to go and save you, Arthur, at any cost. For this purpose she gave me your sword Excalibur and the scabbard." Before the knight could say anything further Arthur understood each and everything. He knew that the real culprit was his aunt who had hatched the entire plot to do away with him. He got sad at heart having known so much about his dear aunt. He said to the knight, "I shall teach my aunt a lesson later on. But before that I must take revenge upon Sir Damas."

Arthur said to Sir Accolon, "Get ready for making on attack on Sir Damas. I won't spare him for locking me up in his cell." Along with Sir Accolon and three other knights Arthur led an attack on Sir Damas. A great battle was fought. At last Arthur registered a victory over Sir Damas. All his soldiers were put to death mercilessly. In doing so Arthur got badly wounded. But he had won the battle handsomely. Sir Damas was put behind bars. Arthur went to see him in his cell. He asked Sir Damas, "How do you feel here? Now, you shall remain here throughout your life. Tell me the truth who told you to do so? In case you speak me truth, maybe I can release you. In case you tell a lie, you will face dire consequences. So, be careful before speaking anything."

Sir Damas thought in his heart of hearts, 'It is the best opportunity to save my life, otherwise the wrath of Arthur will put me to death.'

Thinking thus he stated, "Your aunt Morgan le Fay told me to do so. She wants to usurp the throne. She wants her son to sit on the throne of Britain. That is why she hatched all the plot."

Hearing the words Arthur's eyes welled up. He loved her aunt so much. It is said that everything is fair in love and war. Arthur's aunt was no exception. Under the pretext of a close relative Queen Morgan Le Fay tried to put an end to Arthur. But mysterious are the ways of God. He had something else in store for Arthur. Now Arthur said to Sir Damas, "You are no knight, O Sir Damas. There is no need for you to have your sword and shield."

Thereupon Arthur shattered Sir Damas sword and shield. He also impounded all his movable and immovable property and handed it over to his younger brother.

After handing over the property of Sir Damas to his younger brother, Arthur headed for Camelot. There at Camelot a spy presented himself before Morgan le Fay. After paying his obeisance to the Queen the spy said, "O dear Queen! Here is bad news for you. Arthur is still alive. He has overcome all obstacles. Moreover, he has handed over all the property of Sir Damas to his younger brother. He is on his way back to Camelot. Sir Damas has revealed everything to him. Arthur is in sultry mood. None can stop his anger from venting out."

Hearing the words of the spy the Queen trembled with fear. She knew Arthur would not spare her life. She let the spy go. After the spy had gone away, Morgan le Fay thought, 'I had better go back to my kingdom as quickly as possibly. Before Arthur reaches here, I shall be away to my kingdom. This is the only way whereby I can save my life.'

The Queen went over to Queen Guinevere, with whom she was residing, and stated, "O dear friend! I think it is time for me to return to my kingdom. I have been here for many days. My subjects are missing me very much. I must go back to my country."

Hearing the words of Morgan le Fay Queen Guinevere observed, "O dear, you need not worry about your subjects. Everything is OK there. King Arthur is on his way back to Camelot. He will be extremely happy to see you here."

But Morgan le Fay was very much terrified in her heart of hearts. On the other hand, Queen Guinevere did not know at all what Morgan le Fay had done. So, she kept on insisting on her stay there in Camelot. But Morgan le Fay had something else in her mind.

After a while she said to Queen Guinevere, "O dear, I can't stay any longer. I have to go back to any country. My countrymen are beckoning me. They are in great distress." Saying these words she mounted on her black horse and rode off hurriedly. After Morgan le Fay had left, Queen Guinevere said to herself, 'I doubt the Queen's words. There must be something wrong at the bottom. The time will tell what the matter is?'

After riding on horseback for a while Morgan le Fay said to herself, 'Arthur is still alive. It is really bad news. This thorn must be done away with as quickly as possible. I won't spare his life this time. I must desire some tactics so that I may put an end to him. In fact, the Queen wanted to bring more harm to Arthur. Her evil mind was not ready to admit that Arthur was still alive. With the intention of bringing more harm to Arthur he contacted many different persons and asked each of them about Arthur. Whenever she spoke, she asked the same questions, 'Where is King Arthur? Where can I find King Arthur? Can you tell me the way where King Arthur has been putting up?' At last, she met an old man and asked him, "Can you tell me the way where King Arthur has been putting up?"

Hearing the words of Morgan le Fay the old man replied, "O dear lady, for your kind information King Arthur has been out of sorts for many days. During his bitter fight with Sir Damas he had been badly wounded. He had a terrible fight at the castle of Sir Damas. Now he is recuperating at the House of the Good Women."

Good Women was an institution which worked for

the poor, the downtrodden, the ailing and the unfortunate. Actually, it worked in the name of God. Its motto was–'service to mankind is service to God.' Many unfortunate people sought refuge in Good Women. It received aids from other countries as well. After gathering information from the old man about king Arthur Morgan le Fay rode on in the direction of Good Women. After a journey of a few hours she reached the house. She tethered her horse to a tree at some distance from the house. Before going inside she changed her clothes and pretended herself to be a hungry lady. She went inside. She came across a fat woman. She said to her, "I am a poor lady. Would you provide me with something to eat? I have not eaten anything for days together. I have heard that yours is a noble institution which works for God and serves the poor. Be kind enough to give me some food."

Hearing the pathetic words of Morgan le Fay the fat woman brought food for her. After eating the food Morgan le Fay rested there for a while. Then, she stated, "Is there anybody else putting up in the Good Women? I have heard that King Arthur has been recovering from his wounds here. Am I right in thinking so?"

The fat woman replied, "There is a person putting up here. If I am not mistaken, he is none other than King Arthur, as the people say. But he is resting right now. It is not the right time to disturb him."

Morgan le Fay thought for a while and hit upon a plan. She observed, "I have nothing to do with King Arthur. I have no spare time. I can't stay here even for a minute to speak to him. But only once, I want to have a look at his face. He is very noble and benevolent. He takes care of his subjects." Morgan le

Fay went on praising King Arthur in a flattering tone, "He is good at heart. He is ever ready to lend a helping hand to the poor, the downtrodden and the unfortunate. He is very great. None in this entire world can equal him in benevolence. He can't see anybody in distress. May God grant him all the riches of the world! May God grant him longevity! Let me have a look at his sweet gentle face. I love him from the core of my heart. He is the darling of everybody. He is the apple of everybody's eyes."

Morgan le Fay praised King Arthur to the skies to win the confidence of the fat lady. It worked in favour of Morgan le Fay. The fat lady observed, "I allow you to have a look at his face. But remember, don't wake him up. He is sleeping soundly. I am in charge of the Good Women. It is my duty and responsibility to look after the persons who seek refuge in this institution."

Morgan le Fay thus promised the fat lady, "I give you word that I won't disturb his sleep. I shall have a look at his face from some distance. I will not wake him up."

The fat lady replied, "OK, you may go inside. Please go this way."

After taking permission of the fat lady Morgan le Fay went inside the room silently. As soon as she entered the room, she found Arthur sleeping in one of the corners of the room. His right hand was badly wounded. It has been bandaged. There were a few scars on his face. Arthur was sleeping soundly. He had his right hand on the Excalibur–his magic sword. The scabbard of the sword was lying at his feet. Morgan le Fay looked around. It was not possible for her to steal Arthur's sword as he had her right hand on it.

Morgan le Fay tried her level best to take away Arthur's magic sword but all her efforts proved an exercise in futility. If she had been able to make Arthur part with his sword, it would have been difficult for Arthur to win over his enemies. Morgan le Fay thought hard and hard, but nothing worked in her favour. At last, she thought, 'I should take away the scabbard of this sword. It is no less than magical. Once it is away, half of the power of Arthur will be gone.'

Thinking so, she moved towards the bed and lay her hand on the scabbard which was lying at the feet of King Arthur. Having got the scabbard in her hand Morgan le Fay felt extremely elated. She was on cloud nine. She was happy in her heart of hearts. She said to herself, 'Now I see what Arthur does without the scabbard. He will be like a rudderless ship.

Morgan le Fay was wearing a long cloak. She hid the scabbard inside the cloak lest the fat lady should notice it. Without wasting a single moment she came out of the room hurriedly and tried to slip out from there. But the fat lady was all alert and on guard. She asked Morgan le Fay, "Have you seen the face of Arthur? Is he still asleep? I think you didn't disturb him."

Morgan le Fay politely replied, "Yes Madam, Arthur is sleeping soundly. I have not disturbed him at all. I have kept my word. I must go now. I am getting late."

The fat lady stated, "If you so wish, you can stay here for a longer time. You can meet him when he wakes up."

"No, I must go on," replied Morgan le Fay.

Taking leave of the fat lady Morgan le Fay hurriedly mounted on her black horse and rode off as quickly as possible. Her horse ran with the speed of the wind.

The fat lady had sort of a forgetful nature.

After Morgan le Fay had departed, Arthur woke up. No sooner did he see the scabbard missing than he was alarmed. He at once got up from his bed, though he was not fully recovered. He cried out in utter pain, "I am ruined. Someone has robbed me of my scabbard." He came outside and asked the fat lady, "Dear Madam, did anyone come into my room, when I was sleeping? My scabbard is missing. I suspect some foul play. Tell me quickly."

The fat lady had sort of a forgetful nature. She thought hard and hard. At last, she was able to recollect. She said to Arthur, "Now I can recollect fully. A lady by the name of Morgan le Fay arrived here a short while ago. She seemed to be poor to me. She begged some food as she was utterly hungry. I gave her food to eat. Then, she requested me to have a look at your face. She praised you to the skies. However hard I tried to stop her from seeing your face, I could not dissuade her. At last I permitted her to look at your face from some distance. After she had looked at your face, she hurriedly mounted on her black horse and rode off with the speed of the wind."

Hearing the words of the fat lady, Arthur got alert. He knew very well that it was none other that Morgan le Fay, who had taken away the scabbard. He asked the fat lady where Morgan le Fay had gone. Pointing to the north, she uttered, "Arthur, Morgan le Fay has gone this way. She is on a black horse. She is wearing a long cloak. I hope she has not gone very far off. You can catch up with her."

Before going after Morgan le Fay Arthur very politely said to the fat lady, "O dear madam, I thank you from the bottom of my heart. I thank you sincerely for having me here in your house. I thank you for looking after me and for taking care of my every need. You have been very good to me all through my stay here. May God grant you longevity! Now I can't stay here any longer. Morgan le Fay has taken away the scabbard of Excalibur, my magic sword. I have to get it back from her at any cost. I must move on."

But the fat lady insisted on his staying there for some more time. She said to Arthur, "Dear! Please don't go away. You are not fully recovered. You wounds have not healed up as yet. Do stay here for a few days. Then, you will be hale and hearty again."

But Arthur didn't pay any heed to what the fat lady said. She could not make him stay there. After taking leave of the fat lady Arthur mounted on his swift horse and rode off in the direction of Morgan le Fay. Soon his horse ran with the speed of the wind.

After half an hour Arthur reached the bank of a river. He looked around. He didn't see anybody whom he could ask Morgan le Fay's whereabout. All of a sudden, he sighted a man who was bathing in the river water. His cows were grazing in a field near by. When the man came out of the river after taking his bath, Arthur asked him, "O dear, please tell me whether anybody has come this way or not. I am after a woman on a black horse. She has taken away my scabbard by stealth. She is a bad woman. She has brought slur on the name of my dynasty."

Arthur went on saying, "The woman is mean. She tried to have me killed. I am King Arthur. I look after my subjects very well. Please tell me where that woman has gone."

The man at once told Arthur, "O dear king! She is

a very beautiful lady. She is on a black horse. She has gone across the river just a while before. She was in a tearing hurry. She has something very big in her right hand."

Arthur felt very happy to know about the whereabouts of Morgan le Fay. He at once spurred on his horse. Soon the horse ran with the speed of the wind. In a trice, Arthur went across the river, and through a dense forest and up a hill. He rode on and on. From the hill he looked down on the plains. There he noticed Morgan le Fay far away. Now, both Morgan le Fay and Arthur exchanged glances with each other. Having seen Arthur coming behind her Morgan le Fay spurred on her horse and rode quickly over a stony path. Then down a hill to a lake, Arthur was hotly chasing Morgan le Fay. He wanted to get back the scabbard at any cost. He rode down the hill and spurred on his horse in the direction of the lake. In the meantime, Morgan le Fay dismounted from his horse. She looked at the water of the lake. It was black due to a curse inflicted upon it. No animal or bird ever drank the water of this lake. Even the birds did not sing in the trees around this lake. All in all, the lake was discarded by everybody. Morgan le Fay said to herself, 'This is the right place to dump this scabbard. The lake is not visited by anybody, not even by birds and animals. Nobody shall ever come to know about the scabbard.'

Thinking so, Morgan le Fay with all her might flung the scabbard far right in the middle of the lake. The scabbard being heavy sank into the black water of the lake.

Then she cried out in a loud voice, "Hurrah! I have made Arthur part with his scabbard. Now, he shall never have it. I have completed my mission. Now I see how he wins over his enemies. Without the scabbard he will not be able to save himself from his enemies. It is all over for Arthur. He won't be able to defeat me, however hard he may try." Saying these words Morgan le Fay departed from there riding on her black horse.

After she had left Arthur came to the same spot. But he found none. There was nobody else as far as his eyes could reach. He was there all alone. There was no Morgan le Fay for whom Arthur had arrived there. There were no traces of her horse's hooves because it was a stony path. Arthur felt disappointed and dejected. He sat on a stone, unhappy and forlorn.

All of a sudden, an old man came over there. He patted Arthur's back and said to him, "O dear! Arise and awake. Why are you sitting alone here? Morgan le Fay has gone back to her country. As far as the scabbard is concerned it has been thrown into the black water of this lake. You can never find it. So, go back home and make planning for future." Saying these words the old man disappeared in a trice.

Arthur felt as if he had seen a dream. But it was reality. He had parted with the scabbard for ever.

Arthur Welcomes Lancelot

Sad and desolate, Arthur returned to his country. After reaching his country, he rested for a few days. He didn't go hunting or shooting wild animals for pleasure. He remained at home all through these days. His wounds had healed up. He was up and doing as before. He turned hale and hearty once again.

One morning Merlin the great magician came over to him. He stated, "O Arthur! I thank God that you have fully recovered from your wounds which were very deep. None in this world can harm you till you have the Excalibur. Never part with the sword even for a second. I think you are fully active to launch an attack."

Hearing the words of Merlin Arthur was amazed. He asked him in wonder, "What attack are you talking about?"

Thereupon Merlin observed, "The Saxons and the rebel knights in the north are raising their heads. It is high time that they should be crushed completely, otherwise they will launch an attack on us."

Arthur nodded in the affirmative. He called out his minister and said to him, "Prepare the army for an attack on the Saxons and the rebel knights. They are raising their ugly heads in the north. Before long, they should be taught a bitter lesson."

Next day, at the head of a large army of his brave

knights, Arthur waged a war on the Saxons and the rebel knights. After a gruelling fight against them, he could manage to win over them. He returned to his kingdom with full of joy. His subjects greeted him warmly. Many people garlanded him and congratulated him on his great success.

Days rolled by followed by weeks and months. One day, Arthur was sitting in his court. He called out to his minister and stated, "Dear! We have achieved victory over the Saxons and the rebel knights by dint of hard work and perseverance. Why not hold a joust to celebrate this victory? What do you say in this regard?"

The minister thought for a while. Then, he uttered, "Your Highness! It is a great idea. The celebration should be grand. Everybody should know that we have come out victorious in this bloody battle. You are absolutely right in thinking so."

Thereupon Arthur observed, "Then send out invitation cards to each and every ruler, ruling in and around Britain. Remember this will be a grand celebration. No prominent ruler should be left out. After all, it is the celebration of our victory over the Saxons and the rebel knights."

The very next day, the minister started sending out invitation-cards in hordes. The messengers fanned out in all the direction to distribute the invitation-cards. Soon, the day of the tournament came. Rulers from far and near came to the tournament field. It was a bright sunny afternoon. The tournament field had been bedecked with flags all around. People in hordes came to the field to witness the joust which was a major attraction for young and old alike.

First of all, athletics took place, followed by wrestling

and archery contests. These contests were admired by all the people as no foul play was observed. Arthur himself presented the awards to the winners of these contests. There was one more contest to be conducted before jousting. It was a javelin-throw contest. Many mighty knights participated in this contest. Each performed better than the other.

It was quite difficult for Arthur to declare the winner. After many ifs and buts the winner was declared at last. Later on, Arthur gave him position in his army. The jousting contest was to be conducted now. Everybody present there was eagerly waiting for the contest as the knight who would win was to be announced the queen's champion. Bugles were sounded. Thereafter, a fanfare of trumpets proclaimed that King Arthur would open the contest. One interesting thing in the contest was that King Arthur himself took part in this contest. He was there to give a challenge to each and every knight. This way, he would be able to assess his strength and physical power. In no other contest did Arthur participate. Jousting was very dear to him. He was quite skilled in playing the game of joust. The jousting contest began on a high note.

Arthur wearing his new silver armour sat on his white horse at one end of the field. He had his helmet on. He had a joust in the right hand. Several knights came there to fight against him. But he kept on crushing knight after knight. No knight dared to stand before him even for five minutes. The people cheered their king loudly. They had full faith in their king's valour. They knew it was next to impossible for anyone to defeat their King in jousting. In the pavilion of the distinguished guests, Sir Kay and Sir Bedivere were also sitting. After

Arthur kept on defeating knight after knight.

Arthur had defeated each and every knight in jousting. Sir Kay said to Sir Bedivere, "I bet you none other that Arthur will be the queen's champion. It is next to impossible to make him lick dust. He is very agile, active and alert. He has mastered this form of fighting."

Arthur kept on defeating knight after knight. None of the knight dared to stand before him even for a minute. All of a sudden, a queer silence spread over the tournament field. An extraordinary knight had arrived on the tournament field. All present there were amazed. They had never seen such a knight before in their life. People began to whisper. Seeing the knight Sir Kay said to Sir Bedivere, "Isn't he a strange knight? His armour is plain, and his shield and helmet don't bear a crest. I doubt he is a knight in the real sense. He can't defeat Arthur the mighty."

Hearing the words of Sir Kay Sir Bedivere observed, "Still waters run deep, O dear. Barking dogs seldom bite. Who knows he can defeat Arthur and make him lick dust? If I am not mistaken, he had come here to give a tough fight to Arthur. It won't be easy for Arthur to crush him down like he crushed other knights. Things don't seem easy this time."

There was an atmosphere of amazement in the crowd. Everybody wanted to know who the knight was, where from he had come, who his parents were. One person in the crowd said, "Look, this knight seems to be mighty and powerful like our own King Arthur. He seems to be an equal match for our king. It will be a very interesting tussle between the two. It is said when two bulls fight, it is the grass that suffers. If this knight is able to defeat our King, will he be declared our new King? Are we going to suffer on this count? No, this can't happen. Let us cheer our King and pray to God that our King Arthur should come out victorious, come what may. Who knows how the new knight will rule over us in case he wins the tournament."

In the meantime the new knight sitting on his white horse came to the battlefront. He raised his lance in order to salute King Arthur and other dignitaries present there. Thereafter, he spurred on his horse and rode towards King Arthur. On the other side, Arthur too was very excited to measure arms with that extraordinary knight. He got himself ready to attack the knight. From one end, the knight with a lance in his right hand rushed towards Arthur. From the other end, Arthur too rushed in the direction of the knight. He too had a sharp lance in his right hand.

As the two came close to each other, their lances struck with a loud crash. It broke their lances. But both of them were sitting firmly on their horses. Neither of them was rendered unhorsed. Both were equally powerful and mighty. Each was trying his level best to overcome the other. Now both the knights exchanged glances with each other. After their lances had come to the pieces, each of them picked up a new lance. They again rode back. Reaching the starting point from each end, both of them again took a start. Coming each other's way their lances again clashed. It again resulted in a loud crash.

It yielded the same result. Again, their lances broke into two pieces. The crowd was amazed to see this strange sight. None was able to understand what was going on. Sir Kay said to Sir Bedivere, "Dear friend, what I told you before the start of the joust. This knight is not an ordinary knight. He is very much skilled in wielding a lance. He is equally powerful and agile. Let us see what takes place ahead." Sir Bedivere saw eye to eye with Sir Kay.

Now, both Arthur and the knight got down from their respective horses and began fighting with their swords. King Arthur was good at sword-fighting. But the knight was equally good. It was rumoured that King Arthur would win the sword fighting. There ensued a bitter fight between the two. Both the warriors fought for long horse, with mighty blows dealt on either side. All of a sudden, King Arthur raised his sword above his head. He said to the unknown knight, "Enough is enough. I have now come to the conclusion that neither of us can be defeated. You are equally strong and agile. It is not fair that I should be selected champion at arms to my lady, the queen. You too deserve this honour. You are really worthy of it. Let me know who you are and where from you have come. I kindly request you to make yourself known to all of us. We are eagerly looking forward to your identity. Please reveal your identity. It is too much. Now, I declare that you are my equal in sword-fighting."

Hearing the words of King Arthur the knight dismounted from his horse. With both palms joined in utter reverence he said to King Arthur, "Your Majesty, I am Lancelot of the Lake. I hail from France." Saying these words the unknown knight took off his helmet.

Lo and behold! It was the handsome face of a young lad no longer older than King Arthur himself. Everybody present there was all praise for the knight. After all, he had given a tough battle to Arthur. The crowd cheered the new knight who felt elated and excited. King Arthur had now realized that there were knights still more powerful and agile than he himself was. He welcomed

*Lancelot was presented Sash around
his shoulders by Queen Guinevere.*

64

the new knight warmly. After the introduction King Arthur said to the knight, "What brought you to Camelot?"

Lancelot replied at once, "Your Majesty! I had heard of the Fellowship of Knights that you formed some time ago. I have come over here to become a knight of the Round Table. That is why I showed you my mettle and grit. What do you say now?"

King Arthur was all praise for Lancelot. He stated, "Dear, you have earned a place for yourself in the Fellowship of Knights by dint of hard work and perseverance. From today onwards you are appointed to the Fellowship of Knights." Saying these words King Arthur embraced Lancelot to his bosom and proclaimed him Champion at arms of the queen. Lancelot felt extremely happy to get this rare honour.

Next day, Lancelot was presented Sash around his shoulders by Queen Guinevere. When Lancelot looked at the Queen, he fell in love with her as she looked the most beautiful woman on earth he had ever seen. He smiled a little other bit and both exchanged glances with each. From that very day, he swore to himself that he would serve the Queen for as long as he lived. On the other hand, Queen Guinevere too fell in love with Lancelot. It was love at first sight for each of them. Only Merlin was aware of the love between the fair Queen and Lancelot. The seeds of love had sprouted in each heart. But Merlin felt sad as he knew that their love would cause the rupture of the Fellowship of the Round Table many years later. It was against the ethics of the Round Table. But Merlin had no alternative but to keep mum. He did not let this thing reveal to anybody else. He kept the sorrow in his heart. He left everything to the fate.

Gareth Marries Linet

In due course, Sir Lancelot became the finest and efficient knight of the Round Table. He had all the virtues of being a true knight. He was gentle, brave, handsome and chivalrous. All the other knights respected him a lot and looked up to him for any kind of help or clarification. He was very just. He never tortured any innocent person. He assisted the captive ladies in running away from the captivity of the evil men. He did away with the giants and the wicked persons. He always lent a helping hand to those who wanted his help.

One fine morning, King Arthur was holding his court. All his knights at the Round Table were sitting there. Queen Guinevere too sat beside the King. All of them were discussing the future course of action. Even the Queen was putting forward her suggestion. The knights were all praise for their King and the Queen. All of a sudden, a messenger entered the court and said to the King, "Your Highness! A good looking young man has come into the palace. He wants to see you right now. He has not revealed his identity."

Hearing the words of the messenger King Arthur observed, "Bring him in with all respect, O messenger."

The messenger went away and came in again along with the gentleman. Seeing the gentleman King Arthur said to him, "O young lad! Who are you? Where from have you come? What do you want?"

With both palms joined in utter reverence the young lad of eighteen observed, "Your Majesty! I can't tell you who I am. But I need three gifts from you. If you are generous enough, grant me my three gifts. I have heard much about your name and fame. Let us see what you do today."

Hearing the words of the lad King Arthur got surprised. He did not know the lad at all. How could he grant him his three gifts? So, he stated, "Dear, first tell me who you are and where you have come from."

But the lad was not at all ready to tell his name until and unless his three gifts were granted. So, he said to the king, "O King, first promise me that you would grant me my three gifts. Only then shall I tell you about my three gifts."

Thereupon, King Arthur promised the lad that he would do as the lad wanted. After a while the young lad stated, "Your Majesty! Let me wine and dine along with you here regularly for one year. As for my other two gifts, I shall tell you about them two years henceforth. What do you say now? Are you ready to comply with my first request? I hope you won't deny this."

King Arthur thought for a while and observed, "O young lad! I feel disappointed at your modest request. You can ask for something better. Why don't you ask for something else? I can provide you with a lot of comforts here in my big palatial house. Without any doubt, I shall provide you with food and drink. I have not denied that to anyone, not even to my enemies. After all, you are my guest and I am you host. So, it becomes my first and foremost duty to provide you with the best of food and drink. Please tell me your name."

The young lad thought for a while and stated thus, "Your Majesty! I beg your pardon for this. I can't tell you my name. I can't do this, Your Majesty. Please forgive me for this. I am bound by some condition. Please do cooperate with me."

Sir Kay was sitting there. He did not like the way the young lad had replied to the king.

Sir Kay was a man of hot temper. He felt irritated a lot. He wanted to punish the young lad for his impudence. He said to King Arthur, Your Highness! This man seems to be a fool to me. He harps on the same tune. How can he have his own say? He is interested only in eating and drinking. He can't be capable enough in becoming a knight of the Round Table. To me he looks like a spy who has come over here for extracting information from us. Beware of this false man, Your Majesty. I doubt his intention of coming here. Had he been a true knight, he would have asked you for a horse and armour. He would have asked you for a sword and its sheath. He would have asked you for a shield. He would have asked you for a javelin. But this is not so. He seems to be some farm boy. Appoint him in the kitchen. There, he will get plenty to eat and drink. In a year's time, he will gain weight and become as fat as a swine. But I am not at all in favour of his being appointed here in this palace of ours."

Hearing the words of Sir Kay all the knights sitting there spoke in one voice, "Yes, Sir Kay is absolutely right. Maybe he has come over here to get some important information. We all are not in favour of his being appointed here. Expel him from the hall right now."

King Arthur was silent. Before he could say anything Sir Lancelot who had been recently appointed knight of the Round Table spoke in favour of the young lad. He was not at all satisfied with the way Sir Kay had spoken about the youth.

Sir Lancelot got up from his seat and thus addressed the gathering, "O great knights and King Arthur! Much has been said about this young lad who is completely innocent. As he is very young he has not asked for a horse and armour, as Sir Kay mentioned a while ago. He is too young to ask for things or equipment related to warfare. But look at the splendour as this young lad's forehead. He promises to be a great honourable man in future. Then at that time we all shall look foolish in front of him. If I am not mistaken, he is going to be a man of great honour. O King, do allow him to eat and drink with us. This man can't be an enemy spy." A strange thing happened.

Hearing the words of Sir Lancelot the young lad got very happy. He was all praise for him with both palms joined in utter reverence he said to Sir Lancelot, "Sir, thank you for supporting me in this grand assembly. You are the only one who has supported me. But I beg your pardon. I would like to do as Sir Kay wants me to do. I shall work in the kitchen with the other boys for one whole year. If Your Majesty permits me to do so, I shall be more than happy." He told the king that his name was Gareth.

King Arthur without thinking far a moment permitted the young lad to work in the kitchen for one whole year. So, throughout the long year the young man worked in the kitchen with the other boys. He ate and drank as and when he wanted. There were no restriction on him. He relished the food and drink he liked very much. After one year had elapsed, the young man as

Hearing the pathetic tale of Linet
King Arthur had all sympathy for her.

he had promised King Arthur came into the hall. King Arthur was sitting with his knights.

When the young lad reached in front of the King, he saw a beautiful young lady standing there. She was extremely beautiful. Seeing the lady the young lad fell in love with her. It was love at first sight. Her name was Linet. With both palm joined in utter reverence she said to the King, "O your Majesty! My name is Linet. I have come here on purpose. I live on the outskirts of Britain. Last night four knights barged forcefully into our house and took away my beautiful sister. Their names are Morning, Noon, Evening and Night. We are only two sisters and we live our life seeing each other. Now without her how can I live life? So help me, otherwise I will end my life."

Hearing the pathetic tale of Linet King Arthur had all sympathy for her. He said to the young lady, "O dear, don't worry. Your sister will be at home soon. Rest assured none can harm your sister in any way."

Linet thanked the king and stated, "Your Highness! Please send one of your knights to rescue my sister. I am in favour of Sir Lancelot. He is brave and chivalrous. He can easily did away with the abductors."

Before King Arthur could order Sir Lancelot to go and rescue Linet's sister the young man stepped in. He said to the King, "Your Majesty! I am very much pleased with your hospitality. You have provided me with food, drink and shelter for one whole year. Thanks a lot for this from the core of my heart. My words fail me to express my indebtedness to you. Do me one more favour. Please grant my second gift—the opportunity to show you my valour. Please send me on this adventure. Don't refuse, please." King Arthur thought for a while. He then observed, "So be it! If you are interested in rescuing Linet's sister, I have no objection to it, provided you must have enough courage to do this feat."

The young lad felt extremely elated. But Linet was not at all happy with the King's decision. She was interested in Sir Lancelot. So, she got very much angry with the young lad. Despite her all efforts she failed to bring the king round to her viewpoint. Before mounting on her horse she said to King Arthur, "Your Majesty! I want none other than Sir Lancelot for my help. I have asked for him but you provide me with one of your kitchen boys. What is this nonsense? It is none of his business. I want nothing to do with this kitchen boy."

Saying these words Linet mounted on her black horse and galloped away. Soon, the horse started running with the speed of the wind. King Arthur came up to Gareth and helped him put on his armour quickly. He also provided him with a brilliant sword. He sent his servants to fetch one of his swift horse and helped Gareth ride on it.

Gareth after putting on armour spurred on his horse and rode after Linet. He rode quickly and soon caught up with her. Seeing Gareth ride beside her Linet felt very angry. She refused to speak to him. However hard he tried to speak to her, she always flatly refused to do so. Riding on and on, both Linet and Gareth reached a river-bank. On the far end of the river, there was a red tent. In front of the tent, stood a man in blue armour. His name was Morning whom both Linet and Gareth had been searching for.

Seeing Morning Linet said to Gareth, "O kitchen boy! If you want to run away, you have still the opportunity of doing so. Once Morning reaches here, you will be no more."

But Gareth was not a lad to be cowered down. He

said to Linet, "O beautiful lady! I have lost my heart to you. I can sacrifice my life for you. Even if death stares into my face, I won't run away. I am not scared of anybody. Today I show you who I am and what I can do for you." Saying these words Gareth rode hurriedly across the river and challenged Morning to a sword duel.

The two warriors fought ferociously. Their swords clashed together and made a loud sound that was enough to deafen a person. Lady Linet standing at the other end of the river was fuming with anger seeing all the proceedings. She was not at all happy with the fact that a mere kitchen boy was measuring arms with a knight. The two knights were fighting on their horses with swords.

Soon, they started fighting with their spears. Now, it was a contest of 'do or die'. Even though the young man's shield was cut away from his arm yet he did not lose heart. He kept his cool and continued fighting with great zeal. At last, the young man with all his might succeeding in thrusting his spear into the heart of Morning. Soon, Morning lay slain on the grass at his feet. The contest was over. But lady Linet was not at all pleased with the young lad. Muttering on she rode on her horse and galloped away. But the young lad was bent upon taking revenge.

Soon, he caught up with Linet and stated, "I care a fig what you say or think about me. I have pledged that I shall do away with all your enemies. That is all." Saying these words both rode on. It was extremely hot. The sun was shining with all its brightness. Soon they reached another river.

The river was flowing smoothly. Both of them dismounted from their horses and started looking at the river. All of a sudden the young lad sighted a man across the river. The man, on the other end, too saw him. He was none other than Noon, the second enemy of Linet, whom the young boy was eagerly searching for. Noon from the other end shouted loudly and asked Linet, "Who is this young lad? Why has he come over here?"

Lady Linet replied, "He is a mere kitchen boy. King Arthur has sent him here to fight against you. He has slain your brother Morning. Now he is ready to measure arms with you."

Hearing the words of lady Linet, Noon's blood was boiling with all fury. His eyes became red with blood. He was mad in anger. He yelled at the young lad saying, "O dam fool! Don't you love your life? How dare you do away with my brother? Stay there. I am just coming to teach you a biter lesson." Saying these words Noon who was a terrific swimmer soon swam across the flouring river. Reaching the other end he challenged the young boy to a sword duel. Soon, a ferocious fight between the two ensued. The two lads were all in fury. Fighting on, they jumped into the river and clashed with each other there.

Sometime they got to blows. At other times, they fought with their swords. The young boy wounded Noon four times with his sword. Noon fell off his horse. But he was a man of grit and courage. He was not to be covered down. Soon he got up and rode on his horse. In the meantime Lady Linet kept on taunting the young boy in one way or the other. Soon, both of them came to a hill. From the top the young man looked down on the great river. There, he saw another man. He at once understood that he was none other than Evening. The very next moment he thrust his sword into Noon's heart. Noon died there and then.

Lady Linet was still not happy at all. She was not ready to accept the fact that a mere kitchen boy was doing away with all his enemies one by one. The young lad came down the hill towards the man whom he had seen from the top. As the young lad rode nearer, he saw that the man's armour was red in colour. There was a picture of a red evening sun on his shield. The young man lost no time in understanding that he was face to face with his third enemy. The man on the other hand sighted Gareth's shield. He saw the picture of the golden sun on it. He yelled joyously, "Hey brother! What brings you here? You are most welcome in my territory. Come Noon! I welcome you from the core of my heart."

It so happened that before killing Noon Gareth the young boy had snatched his shield. That was why Evening mistook Gareth for Noon. But Lady Linet interrupted saying, "No he is not Noon. He is his murderer. He has done away with two of your brother. Now he has come over here to kill you. Beware of this young man!"

Hearing the words of Lady Linet Evening was red in anger. His eyes were bloodshot. He was fuming with anger. He soon took out his sword and challenged Gareth to a sword fight. Both got to fighting soon. Gareth mollified every attack of Evening. But Evening could not face Gareth, who was more courageous. Soon, Evening's sword broke into two pieces. Gareth snatched his shield. Now Evening was unarmed. He lay prostrate at the feet of Gareth and asked for his forgiveness. But Gareth did not want to pardon him. So, he asked Linet, "O sweet lady, what do you say? Should I forgive him? If you wish so, I shall give him a new lease of life."

Lady Linet thought for a while and then answered,

"I have nothing to say in this matter. It is up to you. If you are not a coward, kill him at once."

Hearing the words of Lady Linet Gareth raised his sword in the air to kill Evening but Evening began to weep bitterly. He asked for his forgiveness. The milk of human kindness flowed through Gareth's heart. He pardoned him. Evening thanked Gareth and told him the way to the castle wherein Night, his brother, had imprisoned Lady Linet's sister.

Seeing the generosity of Gareth lady Linet was filled with sympathy for Gareth. She was all praise for him. Now she had been changed to a noble lady. Seeing the noble nature of Gareth she was greatly impressed by him. She said to Gareth, "O dear, you are so noble, great and sympathetic. I have always taunted you, called you names and denounced your action. But I didn't know that you are very kind at heart. Please forgive me, if you can. I too love you. I want to marry you."

Hearing the words of Lady Linet Gareth observed, "It is never too late to mend. I forgive you. But one this is sure. Had you not spoken rudely to me from time to time, I would not have been able to fight to my fullest potential. Yes, it is very much true that your unkind words did make me angry, but they encouraged me to fight even more fiercely. So, I thank you for this. Let us be true friends from today onwards."

Hearing the words of Gareth Lady Linet felt extremely happy. She was pleased in her heart of hearts that Gareth had forgiven her for her impudence.

From that day onwards, they became chums. They resumed their journey in the direction of the fourth and last enemy. His name was Night. They rode on and on till they reached a cave. The sun was going down the horizon. Evening approached. They took shelter in the cave. Once inside, Lady Linet made a fire. Both of them warmed themselves sitting near the fire. They ate and drank there. In the meantime, the sun completely went down the horizon. Before long, night came on. After resting for a while, they again rode on. Riding in the south, they reached a castle which was called the castle Perilous.

On the top of the castle a black flag was waving to and fro. There was a black tent in front of the door of the castle. There was a pin-drop silence. It was stark dark. Pointing to the castle Lady Linet said to Gareth, "Dear, this is the castle wherein my sister has been imprisoned. But it is next to impossible to win over him. He is the bravest of all the four. He is the meanest as well. It is said that he equals ten men in strength. I won't ask you to fight this enemy of mine. He is more a monster than a normal human being. Let us run away from here. Leave the fate of my sister to God. He alone can save her from this terrible monster. Come along; all your efforts to save my sister from the custody of this evil rascal will prove to be an exercise in futility."

But Gareth was not a coward. He was courageous. He observed, "Dear, don't worry. Your safety and your sister's is my concern now. I am not scared of this man, however big he is. I believe in the power of God. They say that God sees but waits. I think the time has come when this devil has to meet with his nemesis."

Thus Gareth without being scared of the terrible monster approached the castle gate. There he saw that a horn hung in front of it. He seized the horn and blew it with all his might. Lo and behold! There appeared lights at the windows of the castle. From one of the windows Linet's sister, Lady Lyonors, appeared. She was surrounded by some ladies who had swords in their

Gareth again blew the horn.

hands. Seeing her sister Lady Linet felt very happy. She wanted to meet her, but she was stopped by Gareth lest she should be made hostage. Seeing Gareth, Lady Lyonors bowed to him most majestically.

Gareth again blew the horn. This time, there appeared Night, the devil who had imprisoned Lady Linet's sister. With much fanfare, he appeared at the castle gate. So many guards accompanied him. He had a black armoured rode on a black horse. He was wearing a helmet as well so as not to reveal his identity.

Seeing him Gareth stated, "O devil I am not afraid of your black armour or black horse. If you have the courage of ten men, come on and fight against me. Let us see today which way the wind blows. Let us see who is the stronger of the two." Saying these words Gareth pounced upon Night like a leopard. Seeing his agility even Night was awestruck.

Lady Linet shut her eyes as she did not want to see any harm on the body of Gareth. Both the warriors fought ferociously. All of a sudden, Gareth attacked Night from behind and broke his shield into two pieces. Now Night was unarmed. He was all hands up. Before Gareth could raise his sword to kill Night, he begged his forgiveness. He said to Gareth, "Sir! Please don't kill me. My three brothers made me enact this play. It was all pre-planned. They wanted me to marry Lady Lyonors."

"My brothers were very nice. They did not want that any one else should marry Lady Lyonors. That was why I imprisoned her in this castle while they stopped, everybody from coming near to this palace. As you are brave, you have crossed all the barriers to reach here. You are great. I bow to you."

Saying these words he removed his helmet. Seeing

his innocent face everybody standing there was awestruck. He was a very handsome young boy of twenty-five years of age. Knowing all the truth, Lady Lyonors felt very grateful to Night. She had great respect and love for him.

Soon Linet accompanied by Night and Lady Lyonors entered the castle. There, Linet met her sister. Seeing her safe and sound she was on cloud nine. She embraced her sister and thanked the Almighty for her safety. All of them were in happy mood.

As a matter of fact, King Arthur had had sent Sir Lancelot after the boy. Sir Lancelot had been continuously following the boy throughout their journey. He had now realized that the boy was a brave fighter. He had truly judged his bravery while he put down all the four knights in a trice.

As a mark of respect, Sir Lancelot rode up to the boy and said to him, "O dear you are so great. Hats off to you! You have proved yourself to an unparalleled warrior in any kind of war. Would you like to tell me who you are and where from you have come? I can judge from your fine traits that you are not an ordinary cook. Please let me know about you and your family."

Hearing the words the boy thus spoke out, "Sir, I am Gareth and I am the son of King Lot of Orkney. For your kind information, my brother Sir Garvaine is one of the knight of the Round Table. What more do you want to ask me?"

Hearing the words of the boy Sir Lancelot was more than happy. He was in a state of ecstasy. He knew from the core of his heart that the boy was not a mere kitchen boy. But he was still perplexed as to why the boy did not reveal his identity. So, he asked the boy very earnestly, "Dear, one thing still pesters me. Please let me know why you kept your identity a secret. What was the reason behind it. Please elaborate it in detail."

Thus the boy spoke out, "Sir, right from my childhood I wanted to be a knight and be a knight of the Round Table. But my mother was fully opposed to this idea of mine. When I told her that I was leaving the house, she began to weep bitterly. She agreed to my leaving house on the condition that I should work as a kitchen boy for a full one year. So, I kept my promise. I didn't let anyone know about my real identity. Thus I did not incur the wrath of my mother."

Hearing the story behind the identity of the kitchen boy Sir Lancelot was overjoyed. Lady Lyonors welcomed them all in the castle. Linet was happy in the company of her sister. It was all possible due to the chivalric attitude of the kitchen boy. All were full praise for the boy who was brave as well as handsome. Moreover, he was of noble birth.

Linet in her heart of hearts wanted to marry Gareth. It was love at first sight. Gareth too started loving Linet. Soon they all returned happily to Camelot where they were received warmly by King Arthur. Gareth said to King Arthur, "Your Highness! Time has come for me to ask you for my third gift. Let me be a knight of the Round Table henceforth."

Arthur gladly gave the gift to him and made Gareth a knight of the Round Table. Gareth married Linet and thus became her life partner for ever.

Geraint Wins the Golden Falcon

King Arthur was passing his days peacefully. One day, he was sitting in relaxed mood. He called one of his ministers and said to him, "Now there is peace and tranquility in my kingdom. My subjects are happy and contended. I have a mood to go out somewhere tomorrow morning."

The minister joining both his palm with great reverence spoke out thus, "Your Highness! Why not take a ride in the forest? This time of the year is good for riding in the forest. If you order, I shall get ready your horse for tomorrow's excursion."

After thinking a while King Arthur said, "O dear, it is a good idea. A long time has elapsed since I saw the scenery and beauty of the forest. Get ready my men and horses. I will go riding in the forest tomorrow morning."

Queen Guinevere who was sitting beside the King iterated that she too would accompany the King.

Next day, Queen Guinevere could not wake up on time. So, the King along with his men and horses left for the forest. Now there were only two horses left. So, Queen Guinevere took one of the maids with her. Both of them rode on their respective horses and headed for the forest. As the queen was on her way, she heard someone coming. She halted to see who he was. She looked back and saw that he was none other than Geraint, one of the knight of the Round Table. He was unarmed as he had been with the King who was going to the forest. Moreover, he was dressed for riding in the forest. All of a sudden, Queen Guinevere noticed a gold-handled sword at the side of Geraint seeing the queen the knight with both his palms joined in utter reverance bowed before her and welcomed her warmly.

The queen too greeted the knight gaily. After the greeting was over, the queen asked the knight, "How do you happen to be here? You must be with the King at this moment."

The knight most respectfully replied, "Dear Queen! I got up late in the morning. The King had gone riding in the forest. I came to know that you too had gone riding in the forest. As you are alone here, I came here to protect you. That is all."

Hearing the words of the knight the queen felt overjoyed. She said to the knight, "O dear, I respect your devotion and dedication to your duty. We need such knights in our army. Such knights as you scale great heights in their life. I am proud of you and your devotion."

Soon the knight got along with the queen and her maid. They rode on and on until they arrived at a hut. They were very tired and thirsty. They halted there and rode off their respective horses. Then they drank water to quench their thirst. Thereupon they sat there to wait for the King. An hour passed but the King did not go past there. All of a sudden the queen chanced to see a sight which is worth mentioning. At far off distance she heard the sound of the hooves of the horses.

Lo and behold! A knight in full armour rode on a

great war-horse. A richly dressed lady riding on a white stead was following him. Behind the lady, there rode a dwarf who had a violent, bearded face. He was quite ugly. One more strange thing was noticed. On the back of the dwarf there hung the knight's shield. Even more astonishing to the eyes of the onlookers were his both hands. His left hand carried his master's lance whereas his right hand carried a long whip. It was altogether an amazing sight to watch.

Now the queen questioned Geraint, "Can you tell me, O knight, who this knight is, who this lady is and who this dwarf is? Is he too the knight of the Round Table? Does he know King Arthur?"

Thus the queen rained an array of questions upon Geraint who got confused. With great humility he replied, "O dear queen! I can't answer your any of the questions. I am unable to reply as I have not seen the face of the knight. Without seeing his face it is quite hard to tell who he is and whether he belongs to the Round Table or not."

Thereupon the queen turned to her maid and stated, "You go and ask the dwarf who this knight is and who this fine lady is?"

The maid without any opposition went over to the dwarf and questioned him thus, "O dear, can you tell me who this knight is and who this fine lady is?"

The dwarf stood motionless and said nothing. The maid again repeated the question. Thereupon the dwarf hit her hard in the face with a stick. The maid soon returned to the queen and told her thus, "O dear queen! The dwarf is very rude and outrageous. He didn't tell me anything about in spite of my repeated request. At last, he hit me hard in the face and chided me. He also warned me against showing my face to him again.

Hearing the words of the maid Geraint cried out in surprise. He stated thus, "How dare he hit you in the face? I go and see that dwarf. If the need arises, I shall teach him a lesson."

Thus taking the permission of the queen Geraint went over to the dwarf. He spoke to the dwarf in a roaring voice, "Hey you! Can you tell me the name of this knight?"

The dwarf rudely told him, "It is none of your business. You have nothing to do with him. He too has nothing to do either with you or your name."

Hearing the words of the dwarf Geraint flew into a rage. He uttered violently, "Hey you stupid fellow! Don't you know who I am? I have spoken to greater man than your knight is. What does he think of himself. If you don't tell me who he is, I will go and ask myself. I see who stops me from doing so." Saying these words Geraint advanced a little bit in the direction of the knight.

But the dwarf was to alert. He roared violently, "Hey! Stop short or I shall hit you with this whip of mine."

But Geraint, as brave he was kept on moving ahead with taking care of the dwarf's jackal-threat. But the dwarf was not telling a lie. He lifted his whip and hit Geraint in the face with it. Geraint was mad in rage. He stated thus, "O dwarf! How dare you hit me? You are no match for me in bravery."

Saying these words he took out his sword from the sheath. As he got ready to hit the dwarf with the sword, he realized that he would be immediately attacked by the knight if he killed the dwarf. So, he put the sword back in the sheath.

The dwarf made fun of Geraint labelling him a coward.

Seeing this the dwarf made fun of Geraint labelling him a coward. But Geraint did not lose his temper. He kept cool and thought, 'I had better go after the knight. It is no point in measuring arms with him. Moreover, he has armour and I don't have any. Wherever he goes, I will go. I am sure that sooner or later we shall reach some place where I can find armour and fight against him." Thinking so he got ready to go after the knight.

The Queen too supported his viewpoint and observed, "Bravo! Go and kill this knight. If you are not able to kill him, then find out who this knight is and why he has come over here in this dense forest."

Taking permission of the queen Geraint rode after the unknown knight, the lady and the dwarf never allowing himself to be seen, but always keeping them in sight. His horse ran with the speed of the wind. He rode on and on. He rode through fields, forests and rode over hills and across rivers. The journey was quite long. But he did lose heart. He kept his composure and rode on and on like a brave warrior. After two hours' journey he reached a city. The city was very beautiful. There was a big temple on a hill. Beside the hill, there was a huge castle. Geraint was surprised a little bit. He dismounted his horse and looked around. He saw in the street of the city, men were washing armours, putting shoes on horses and sharpening swords and lance points. In fact, they all were making preparations for a joust. Geraint was an ace in the joust-competition.

After taking a stroll around the city he rode on his horse again and headed for the castle on the hill. It took him hardly half an hour to reach at the peak of the hill.

The castle was very big and huge. It was quite

beautiful. The outside walls of the castle had some stones missing. The stones had fallen from the walls. The castle all around was tastefully decorated like a bride. The road to the castle was covered with grass. The door of the castle was broken and old.

All in all the castle seemed to be quite old. There were no guards outside to protect it from invaders. Geraint was somewhat bewildered. He dismounted his horse. He tethered the horse to a nearby tree. Then he approached the gigantic door of the castle. It was closed from inside. He knocked at the door but nobody appeared there. He again knocked at the door but again nobody answered. When he again tried to knock, an old man, all of a sudden, opened the door. From his appearance, he did not seem to be a doorman.

Geraint looked at the old man from head to toe. The old man was wearing the clothes of a knight or a prince. A sword was dangling by his side. He was tall broad and muscular. But his clothes were holes which had been covered by bits of cloth. Geraint was perplexed a lot. The sartorial sense of the old man suggested that he was a knight or belonged to a noble family. But his mannerism suggested something otherwise. All in all, Geraint was non-plussed having seen the old man.

Seeing Geraint in front of him the old man very humbly said to Geraint, "What brings you here O gentleman? May I be of any help to you?"

Hearing the words of the old man Geraint replied, "Sir, I have lost my way. I think I have come far-off from my place. So, I would like to stay here tonight if you permit so. Moreover, I am dead tired and hungry and thirsty. Would you offer me something to eat?"

The old man stated, "O son, I have a little bit to offer

you. Whatever I have, we may equally share. You can stay here tonight. Feel at home and come inside."

Thus the old man showed Geraint in. As soon as Geraint came inside, he saw an old woman sitting in one corner of the house. She was very-very old. Her clothes were torn from many sides. The old woman welcomes Geraint warmly and offered him a stool to sit on. Then, she called out to her daughter, "O dear, a guest has arrived. Please bring food for him. Bring drinks also as he is very thirsty as well.

Soon, a girl by the name Enid brought some food and drinks for the knight. Introducing her to Geraint the old man said, "O fine gentleman, she is Enid, my lovely daughter. In this big castle, she is our only support in our old age. She looks after us well. She has prepared food for you. Please take it and satisfy your hunger."

Geraint looked at Enid from head to toe. She was exceedingly beautiful. Geraint had never seen such beautiful damsel before in his life. He was wonder struck. He had lost his heart to her. In fact, he had fallen in love with her. It was love at first sight. Although her face was pale and her clothes were torn and tattered like those of her parents yet she drew the attention of Geraint.

After Geraint had eaten his meal, he asked the old man, "Sir, please tell me whether this castle belongs to you or somebody else. It is very huge and big."

The old man replied thus, "O son it is a very pathetic tale. We used to be two brothers. We had great love and respect for each other. My brother was blessed with a son. Just after his birth my brother died of pneumonia. Afterwards I brought up his only son with great care and love. As his son grew up, he fell into bad company. By the time he became an ad olescent, he was violent and outrageous. Many a time, he tried to drive me out of this castle. But I kept ground and did not lose heart. Sometime back, he waged a war on me. He took away all the things I had. Even the horses I had were snatched from me. That day onwards I have been living in this huge castle under acute poverty. There is none to help me."

Hearing the pathetic tale of the old man Geraint's eyes welled up. He became somewhat emotional. But he did not show his sentiments to the old man.

Geraint changed the topic and asked the old man, "Sir can you tell me who the knight is who entered the city last evening? With him there are a fine lady and a dwarf. The dwarf has a whip in his right hand and a lance in his left hand. I have been after them. But they have kept themselves hidden somewhere."

The old man thought for a while and told thus, "Dear son, for your kind information the knight's name is sir Edyrn. He is the friend of my brother's son. He is his fast friend. A joust competition is going to be held tomorrow. So he has come here in this city to take part in it. The winner will be awarded a falcon of pure gold. He has been wining the competition for the last two consecutive years. None dares to stand before him. He is very skilful in the art of joust-wielding. I hope this year too he will win the joust competition. Thus he will again win the award of gold falcon."

Hearing the words Geraint roared violently and observed, "Sir, this year he will not win the competition. I shall give him a tough fight for the award. I shall defeat the knight whose dwarf hit the queen's maid and hit me too with his whip. But I am without armour and arms. How will I fight against him?"

The old man went inside a store-room and brought an armour and some arms. He gladly gave them to Geraint who felt extremely happy. But the old man warned Geraint saying, "Dear son, tomorrow's joust needs more than armour and arms. There is one condition attached to the joust competition. Whosoever fights this joust must do so for the lady whom he loves. Can you find the lady whom you love? If you fail to do so, you won't be able to take part in the competition."

Hearing the words of the old man Geraint thought coolly for some time. Thereafter he observed, "Sir, if you don't mind, I would like to tell you something."

The old man spoke out, "O dear son, you are like my own son. So, say without any hesitation. I won't mind it."

Thus Geraint uttered, "If I may do so, I shall fight for your beautiful daughter, Enid. I shall make her my life-partner and be her husband as long as I live. For this, I need your kind permission and your daughter's approval."

The old man readily agreed to what Geraint had asked to do. Enid too happily accepted the proposal of Geraint. In fact, she had fallen in love with him. But she did not let it be known to her father lest he should scold her and marry her off to somebody else. Throughout her life, she had never seen a nobler or more handsome brave knight that Geraint.

Next day, no sooner did the sun rise above the horizon than the old man gave some beautiful but very old armour to Geraint. He also handed over some arms to him. After getting the things Geraint felt overjoyed.

Hearing the words of Geraint Sir Edyrn flew into a rage.

Accompanied by the old man and Enid Geraint headed for the jousting field. Reaching the field Geraint saw that Sir Edyrn was already present there. He was among the crowd. Seeing Geraint he spoke out in a loud voice, "O onlookers! All of you know that I have been winning this competition for the last two consecutive years. My lady is finer, more beautiful than anybody else's. This year too I am going to be the winner without any fail. None has the strength and courage to face my wrath."

Hearing the words of Sir Edyrn Geraint too roared loudly and uttered, "Hey man! Look here. My lady is sweeter and more beautiful than his. Today's joust competition will be mine. I shall be presented with the gold falcon."

Hearing the words of Geraint Sir Edyrn flew into a rage. He was mad like a bull in a bull fighting game. He rode at Geraint and slashed his lance through the helmet of Geraint who fell off his horse. Now Geraint was filled with anger. He humped onto his horse and rode at Sir Edyrn. He let his spear go through Sir Edyrn's shield and Sir Edyrn fell off his horse. People began to cheer the bravery of Geraine. In his next move, Geraine got off his horse and took out his swords. Then he marched towards the falling Sir Edyrn. In the meantime, Sir Edyrn got up and was ready to defend himself. He too took out his sword. Both fell upon each other like two hungry lions. A fierce battle ensued between the two. It was hard to tell who would win the contest. At last Geraint with a quick move of his sword let his sword pierce through the shield of Sir Edyrn. His shield broke in two. Sir Edyrn was without a sword. He was now unarmed. In his next move, Geraint got ready to kill Sir Edyrn there and then. But Sir Edyrn fell at Geraint's feet and begged his forgiveness.

Geraint rebuked him and uttered, "There is no use asking my forgiveness. Go and ask the queen's forgiveness whom your dwarf has insulted. Don't you know she is the queen? You kept on standing and seeing your dwarf's misconduct towards the queen's maid. Why should I spare the life of a knight who is so proud that he insults the queen?"

"But I admit my fault," pleaded the knight, who was filled with fear at the thought of being killed.

Geraint further remarked, "I won't kill you if you go to Queen Guinevere and ask her to forgive you. If she forgives you, you shall live on."

As none of the other warriors were prepared to fight against Geraint he was presented with the gold falcon. The old man and Enid were all praise for Geraint. The spectators too cheered him saying, "long life Geraint!"

Back in the palace of King Arthur, the queen had returned from the forest. After some time, Arthur too had returned from the forest. The queen told King Arthur about everything that happened in the forest—how the knight's dwarf insulted her maid, how the dwarf hit Geraint in the face with his whip. She further remarked, "Your Highness! Geraint has gone after the knight to teach him a lesson."

Next evening, a messenger came up to the King's chamber. With both his palms joined in utter reverence he remarked, "Your Highness! A knight has ridden up to the castle. His shield is broken and he is badly wounded. His helmet is cut in two. It is quite hard for him to sit on his horse. He wants to meet the queen at this very moment. He is in a very pitiable condition."

The King accompanied by the queen went out to meet the knight. The knight was none other than Sir Edyrn. Having seen the queen the knight lay prostrate at her feet. He begged her forgiveness. He uttered, "O queen! I have been badly defeated by Geraint, the brave. He has sent me here to seek your forgiveness. He says that he will spare my life provided you forgive me. Now my life is at your mercy. I admit all my fault. Please forgive me. It is said—do good and forget."

Then he turned to the King and stated, "Your Majesty! Geraint is very brave. You have got a very courageous warrior in the Round Table. Blessed are you and your queen."

Hearing the words of Sir Edyrn Queen Guinevere replied, "I forgive you, O knight. You are free today. Now Geraint will no longer kill you." Saying these words she called some men who took the wounded knight into the castle. The morning after the joust-competition was over. Geraint went back to the old man and said, "Sir, I seek your permission. I must go back to Camelot and meet the King and the queen. They must be waiting for me. I would like to take Enid along with me."

The old man was overjoyed. But soon he became sad. When Geraint asked him the reason for his sadness, he replied, "But Enid has not any beautiful clothes. How will your queen accept her?"

Geraint stated, "Appearances are often deceptive. Never judge a book by its cover, likewise we should judge a person not from his appearance but from his inner qualities." So Geraint and Enid rode back to Camelot. They were indeed very happy.

It was evening. As soon as Queen Guinevere looked

out of the window and saw Geraint, she came rushing out of the castle. She was accompanied by her two maids. She brought both of them inside the palace. Once inside, she said, "Thank you, Sir Geraint, for what you have done. Had it not been your true valour, we would not been able to teach Sir Edyrn a bitter lesson."

Saying so the queen took Enid's hand and led her to her room and gave her one of her own dresses. After wearing the dress, Enid looked all the more beautiful. Whosoever saw her exclaimed in surprise, "She is the most gracious lady we have ever seen."

Thus Geraint and Enid were married with stately pomp and show. The old man got back all that he had lost. So far as his brother's son was concerned, he was exiled by King Arthur.

Brenor Saves the Queen

The subjects were happy with King Arthur and the queen. One morning, King Arthur was sitting in a relaxed mood when one of the messengers appeared in front of him and said, "Your Highness! A man has come to meet you. He is tall and handsome but the coat he is wearing is torn and tattered in many places."

Hearing the words of the messenger the King stated, "Please bring him in with due respect. Let us see what he wants to say to me."

Soon the messenger came back with the man to his side. The man bowed low before the King to pay his respects. King Arthur thus asked the man, "O dear! What do you want from me? What brings you here? Say without any hesitation."

The man with both palms joined in utter reverence said with all humility, "Your Highness! I have heard about the Round Table which is comprised of brave warriors. I too want to be a knight of the Round Table if you permit so."

The King asked the man what his name was. Thereupon the man replied, "Your Majesty! My name is Breunor le Noire. Please make me a knight of your elite Round Table."

Hearing the name of the man Sir Kay, one of the knights of the Round Table, burst into a peal of laughter.

He taunted at the man saying, "We had better call you by the name—the man with the ill-cut coat. That name goes with your dressing up. Your coat is torn in many places. So, this name fits you best. Your real name is a misnomer."

King Arthur interfered saying, "Please be quite, Sir Kay. It does not behove you. One should not make fun of others. So, be a good gentleman."

Turning to the man King Arthur asked him, "Dear! One thing puzzles me very much. Why have you put on a torn coat? What is the reason behind it?"

Thereupon the man related his entire story as follows—

"Long before, my father had gone out for a stroll in a forest. There, as he was dead tired, he fell asleep for an hour. In the meantime, one of his enemies took advantage of this opportunity and attacked my sleeping father. My father while trying to save his life from the enemy got his coat torn in many places. When I came to learn of the attack, I rushed to that place. But it was too late. My father had been killed by the enemy. I had been made an orphan. Since that day onwards, I have been wearing his torn coat which reminds me of his brutal murder. I won't past with this torn coat unless and until I take revenge upon his murderer."

Having heard the pathetic tale of the man the King stated, "Rest assured, I shall make you a knight of the Round Table. But I shall do it tomorrow as the queen along with some knights is going into the garden to pluck some flowers. So, you shall be made a knight tomorrow. By the way, why don't you go along with them? It is a very good garden full of different varieties of flowers. Nature is at its best in the garden. Go and enjoy yourself the scenic beauty of the garden."

Breunor agreed to what King had told him to do. At the head of a large member of knights the queen proceeded towards the garden. Reaching there the queen started taking a stroll around the garden which had different species of roses, lotuses, marigolds etc. At one corner of the garden there were cages wherein different animals had been kept. These cages had been given as presents to King Arthur by different kings. In one of the cages, there was a lion which was trying hard to break open its rusty old cage. None of the knights paid attention to this fact. They all were in the company of the queen.

All of a sudden, the lion roared out loudly and made a last valiant effort to break open the cage. Lo and behold! The cage was broken open by the mighty lion. In one leap, it bounded out. It made straight for the queen who was busy merrily plucking the flowers. None was aware of the lion's presence. Reaching near the queen the lion gave out a loud roar. Having heard the violent roar the queen got terrified. Dropping her bouquet of flowers she ran to save her skin. She ran on and on and hid herself behind a tree. But the lion was bent upon attacking her. It bounded after her. Seeing the unfastened lion, all the knights started running hither and thither. None dared to face the onslaught of the lion as they were unarmed. The queen was left at the mercy of the hungry lion. In a trice, all the knights ran away from the garden to inform King Arthur of the arrival of the lion. But Breaunor, though he was unarmed, stood his ground, unafraid. He blocked the path of the lion and warned it, "O wild beast! You can't harm the queen until and unless you kill me. I won't allow you to do so."

Breunor with all might managed to pierce the sword through the lion's chest.

The lion roared out loudly and uttered, "Be off my way; O gentleman. Don't you love your life? Go and enjoy at home. Let me do my work."

But Breunor was not a sort of man as could be intimidated. He remained there fast to the ground. The lion opened its mouth wide and showed its pointed teeth. Soon, it charged at Breunor. All of a sudden, Breuner sighted a sword which was lying near by. He lifted the sword quickly. In a flash, he struck the lion with it. The lion was badly wounded. But it was not dead. It again charged at Breunor with its all might. Breunor said to himself, 'It is now or never. It I don't kill the lion in this move, it will surely kill me. It is said that a wounded lion is more dangerous than an ordinary lion.'

Breunor with all his might managed to pierce the sword through the lion's chest. The lion writhed about in utter pain and fell down dead. Seeing the lion lying dead on the ground Queen Guinevere came out from her hiding-place. She was very much pleased with the bravery of Breunor. She came near the brave man and patted his back. She told him, "O dear, you displayed great chivalric manner today. Had it not been you, I would have been surely. Killed by this violent wild beast of prey. I owe a debt of gratitude to you."

After the incident the queen along with Breunor returned to the palace. She told king Arthur, "Dear, this young boy is mightier than all your 'knights put together." Saying these words she related the entire incident to the King–How the lion broke open the cage, how all the knights took to their heels having seen the lion and how Breunor risked his life to save hers.

King Arthur felt overjoyed to hear about the bravery

of Breunor. Then, he turned to Breunor and uttered, "O brave warrior! I am proud of you. From today onwards you will be known as Sir Breauner. It means you have joined the elite Round Table."

Hearing the words of the King Breunor thanked the King. His eyes welled up out of happiness. He addressed all the knight thus, "From today onwards I shall not be know as Sir Breunor. Rather, I shall be known as the knight with the ill-cut coat, as Sir Kay suggested it in the beginning. I am grateful to Sir Kay for suggesting me this new unique name."

Thus the story of Breunor came to an end. Throughout his life he was known as a brave knight who single-handedly killed the lion to save the queen.

Sir Meligrance is Killed

The season of summer had set in. Queen Guinevere was fond of flowers. As it was the month of May, the gardens were blooming with beautiful flowers like rose, marigold, lotus, water-lily, sunflower, bougainvillea, etc. The queen desired to go to the gardens and enjoy the scenic beauty and fragrance of flowers. One morning she called her knights and said to them, "O knights of the Round Table! Today I along with my maids desire to go to the gardens to feel the beautiful fragrance of the flowers. There, we shall enjoy the atmosphere and spend some time plucking the flowers. You all will accompany us to give us protection from the enemy."

The ten knights nodded their heads in agreement. A beautiful carriage was decorated for the queen to sit on it. On its both sides, five soldiers each stood guard. Thus the queen's carriage made its way to the gardens where different flowers were in full bloom.

Reaching the garden, the queen got busy in plucking daisies, primroses, roses and marigolds. The queen was very happy that day. The ten knights were following the queen like her shadow. They didn't leave the queen alone even for a minute. Cuckoos, robins and larks were singing melodiously from the trees. Everyone was enjoying himself or herself. Evening had approached. Now it was time to go back to the palace. The queen said to the knights, "It is getting dark now. Let us move back to the palace. King Arthur must be waiting for me. We must hurry up."

As soon as they got ready for their return journey, twenty men in armour and more than a hundred archers came out of the bushes. Their leader, whose name was Sir Meligrance, cried out, "Stop short! If anybody dares to move even a little bit, he/she will lose his/her life. All my archers are skilful. They aim at all of you."

In fact, Sir Meligrance loved Queen Guinevere from the bottom of his heart. Somehow, he could not make her his queen. So, he had a grudge against King Arthur. Now he wanted to outrage the modesty of the queen. So, he wanted to take her away to his castle. Seeing the malafide intention of Sir Meligrance the queen spoke out thus, "Fie! Shame on you! How dare you block our way? King Arthur made you a knight. How can you behave like this with his queen? Aren't you afraid of King Arthur? Don't you know how strong he is? You had better not to incur his wrath. Be off my eyes at once, otherwise you will have to face dire consequences."

But Sir Meligrance was a mean fellow. He uttered, "I care a fig for King Arthur. I am not afraid of him, however mighty and powerful he is. I have always loved you from the core of my heart. Now the time has come when I shall take you away to my castle and marry you. None can stop my way today."

Hearing the words of Sir Meligrance the ten knights spoke out in a body, "Bridle your tongue, Sir Meligrance. Until and unless we are alive, we won't let you succeed in your nefarious act. We shall fight to our last breath. Though we are unarmed and without any armour yet we are ready to face your archers. So what if they have weapons and armour? We have will power and physical strength."

Thereupon Sir Meligrance ordered his archers to shoot their deadly arrows at the knights of the queen. The men of Sir Maligrance let loose their arrows at the unarmed knights of the queen. All the knight lay badly wounded. They were no match for the nighty archers of Sir Meligrance.

Sir Meligrance's archers were wearing armour and carrying spears. They would have killed all the knights of the queen had she not cried out, "I can't see my knights killed before my very eyes. Please stop this bloodshed. I am ready to accompany you to your palace provided you allow me to carry all these wounded knights of mine there as well. In this way, I can take care of their wounds. These knights are like my sons to me. They are very close to my heart. You can't kill them."

Hearing the words of the queen Sir Meligrance ordered his archers to stop shooting at the knights. Thereupon he agreed to the condition of the queen who felt very happy. Thus the wounded soldiers were put onto their horses. Now all of them along with the queen headed for the palace of Sir Meligrance.

On their way, the queen stealthily managed to call her page boy to her side. Then she whispered in his ear, "Go and inform Sir Lancelot of our trouble. Ask him to come over here quickly and save us from the clutches of this evil man."

In a trice, the page boy slipped away from there without being noticed by Sir Meligrance or any of his archers. But fate had something else in store for the queen. As the page boy hurried out, he struck against

The page boy rode on and on, and finally reached the house of Sir Lancelot.

a stone. This made a loud noise which Sir Meligrance heard. He ordered his archers to run after the page boy, as he knew that the queen had sent him for help. However fast the archers ran after the page boy, they could not catch him. Sir Meligrance ordered his archers, "Wait in ambush for anyone who comes here to rescue the queen. As soon as you see someone, shoot at him instantly."

Sir Meligrance quickly reached his castle. On reaching there he had his drawbridge pulled up and the castle door shut completely.

The page boy rode on, and on and finally reached the house of Sir Lancelot. He delivered the entire message of the queen to Sir Lancelot. No sooner did Sir Lancelot hear the message than he flew into a rage. He rode on his horse and marched towards the castle of Sir Maligrance. Soon his horse ran with the speed of the wind. On the way, Sir Lancelot thought, 'I had better go through the forest. Sir Meligrance must have appointed soldiers on either side of the road to attack me in ambush.' Thinking so, Sir Lancelot reached the castle of Sir Meligrance through the forest road. Soon he hid himself in the cart loaded with wood. The cart was going inside the castle. Thus Sir Lancelot without being noticed reached inside the castle. Thereby, he started searching for Sir Meligrance here, there and everywhere.

Sir Meligrance came to learn of the presence of Sir Lancelot inside the castle. He was utterly terrified. He knew none of his soldiers had the guts to face the onslaught of Sir Lancelot. He himself was very scared of Sir Lancelot. So, he hit upon a plan. He went to the queen at once and lay prostrate at her feet. He observed,

"Please forgive me for my guilt. I have done really wrong with you. I must carry you back to Camelot with great honour and safety."

Hearing the words of Sir Meligrance the queen was filled with emotion. She didn't know that Sir Meligrance had seen Sir Lancelot in the castle. She innocently forgave Sir Meligrance for his bad deed. In the meantime, Sir Lancelot reached there and lifted his sword to kill Sir Meligrance. But the queen interrupted saying that she had forgotten him and now it was her duty to save him from any attack. But Sir Lancelot stated, "O queen! Don't come to the rescue of this mean fellow. He is not a good human being. He is a wolf in a sheep's clothing."

But the queen didn't budge an inch from her stand. Now Sir Meligrance knew that Sir Lancelot was very much angry with him in his heart of hearts. So he desired a plan to get rid of Sir Lancelot. At night, a delicious dinner was prepared for the queen and Sir Lancelot. After the dinner, the queen went back to her room to rest. Sir Meligrance asked Sir Lancelot to come along so that he might take him on a round to his castle. Sir Lancelot agreed to take a round, unaware of the nefarious design of Sir Meligrance.

Sir Meligrance took Sir Lancelot from room to room. At last he took him to the armour room. There inside the room a trap was laid. Hardly had Sir Lancelot entered the room when one of his feet got entangled in the trap. Soon, the floor of the room cracked open and Sir Lancelot fell into a dungeon which was very, very dark. Soon the floor shut completely. Thereafter, he returned to the queen and said, "Sir Lancelot has gone back to Camelot. He does not want to stay here any longer."

In the meantime he hid Sir Lancelot's horse on his stable. So, the queen could not know about the reality. After returning to Camelot the queen appeared in front of King Arthur. Seeing the queen and Sir Meligrance together the King was surprised. He said to the queen, "O dear! Did this Sir Meligrance abduct you and take you to his castle. What is the matter? Tell me in detail."

Hearing the words of the King Sir Meligrance lied to the King thus, "Your Majesty! This is all nonsense. I don't have the impudence to do so. I was just playing a joke on the queen. You see the queen has come back, safe and sound."

Then he went near the King and whispered in his ear, "I suspect Sir Lancelot and the queen are in love with each other."

Hearing the nonsensical words of Sir Meligrance the King burst out saying, "You mean fellow! How low can you go? Sir Lancelot when he comes to learn of this nonsense, will not spare your life. Just hold your tongue and stop right now any more of your absurdity."

There in the dungeon, Sir Lancelot was trying every means to get out of there. But all his efforts proved an exercise in futility. A day after he had been put in the dungeon, a girl came there and opened the window door to let he food platter slide in. But Sir Lancelot didn't touch the food. Next day again, the girl came there and again opened the window door to let the food platter in. Sir Lancelot again didn't touch the food. On the third day, the girl again came there. She took pity on Sir Lancelot. She said to him, "O brave Knight! You have been here for the last two days and you have been suffering seriously. Tell me one thing. If I make you free from this dungeon, what will you give me in exchange for you freedom?"

**The moment Sir Lancelot kissed
the girl's forehead, she opened the door.**

Sir Lancelot thought for a while. Then he uttered, "A lady loves gold and diamonds best of all. So, I shall present you gold, silver, diamonds, clothing and what not. I can give you what you can't dream of."

The girl thought for a while and then uttered, "I want nothing. What I want is a gentle kiss on my forehead from a brave warrior, like you, O Sir Lancelot."

Hearing the words of the girl Sir Lancelot was a bit surprised. The girl could have asked for something better and Sir Lancelot would have given in to her. But kissing a lady on the forehead was a simple task. Sir Lancelot replied, "O dear, so be it!" Saying these words he gently kissed the girl's forehead.

The moment Sir Lancelot kissed the girl's forehead, she opened the door of the dungeon. Out came the brave warrior, Sir Lancelot. After coming out of the dungeon on the third day, he felt relieved a lot. He thanked the girl for her kind act and uttered, "Dear! I owe you a debt of gratitude. If ever in life you need something else, please remember me. I shall be with you in an instant."

The girl too was overwhelmed with grief. She observed, "O great warrior! I have never seen such a handsome warrior as you are in my life before. I love you from the core of my heart."

Thus Sir Lancelot found his horse which was tethered to a pole in the stable of Sir Meligrance. He rode on his horse and hurried towards Camelot. There in Camelot, Sir Meligrance had made King Arthur realize that Sir Lancelot was a cheat and he himself was a well-wisher of the King. Sir Lancelot reached the palace where King Arthur along with the queen and Sir Meligrance was sitting in a relaxed mood. No sooner did Sir Lancelot see Sir Meligrance than he flew into a rage. He went near him and caught him by the collar. He said to him in a roaring voice, "O mean and untruthful fellow! What are you doing here? You took away the queen to your castle. Later on, the queen forgave you as you pretended to be innocent. You played a dirty trick on me. You locked me in the dungeon because you wanted me to be your prisoner for life. Last time, I spared your life as the queen insisted on leaving you. But this time, I am not going to spare your life. You will have to meet with your nemesis. I am the strongest of all the warriors of the Round Table. None has the courage to stand before me."

Before King Arthur or Sir Meligrance could say anything, Sir Lancelot took out his sword and pierced it through the chest of Sir Meligrance. All of them standing there were rendered speechless. Sir Meligrance fell down dead there and then.

Holy Grail

One morning, King Arthur along with his queen was sitting in his palace in a relaxed mood. A messenger came inside and said to the King, "Your Highness! An old man dressed in white and with a white beard has come outside. He want to see the Majesty at once."

Hearing the words the King said to the messenger, "Please bring him in with all respect and humility."

Once inside, the old man with both his palms joined in reverence observed, "Long life, our King Arthur! Your Highness! I have brought a young boy to you. He is the son of a great personality. When he grows up, he will earn name and fame. He is expected to do wonderful things for you. Please make him a knight of the Round Table. He will never let you down."

King Arthur looked at the young boy. His face was very beautiful and he was wearing a red armour. The old man led the young boy to the Round Table to the seat Perilous. This seat was something extraordinary. If a true warrior sat on it, the seat would mention his name undoubtedly. The same thing occurred in case of the young boy. As soon as he sat on the seat Perilous, a name appeared on the seat. It was written in gold–Sir Galahad. In fact, no knight had dared to sit on the seat before.

After seating the young boy on the seat Perilous the old man went out and disappeared at once. None saw him where he went. Thereafter, addressing all his knights King Arthur said, "Can anyone of you tell me who this young boy is? He is so fearless, brave and courageous. He dares to sit on the seat Perilous. He is not afraid of anybody. I am amazed at his extraordinary talent."

Sir Lancelot stood up and uttered with all humility, "Sir! I know him, if I am not mistaken. When I rode towards Camelot one day, I came to a house of Good Women. When I was about to leave the house, the Good Women brought out this boy and told me to take him along to Camelot. That is all what I know of this boy."

All the knights sitting there looked at the boy very seriously. They paid a very close look to him. All of them bore some resemblance with Sir Lancelot. At last, they concluded that his face was like that of Sir Lancelot. One of the knights went on saying, "I think he is Sir Lancelot's son. I can recollect that when Sir Lancelot was young, he had married. Out of that marriage he had been blessed with a beautiful brave son. I think he is none other than Sir Lancelot's son."

Thus all the knights as part of conclusion thought, 'Sir Galahad is Sir Lancelot's son. Sir Lancelot knows about this but does not tell anyone.'

But Sir Lancelot did not speak to the young boy as a son. Al the knights were busy discussing the issue. When they heard a loud noise. All became alert lest there should be an enemy. The sound was followed by a great light. It was Holy Grail. All the knights saw that Holy Grail was covered with a piece of red cloth. Soon it had disappeared. Now all the knights felt surprised a lot. They looked at one another but none knew as to where Holy Grail had gone.

Thereupon, Sir Galahad stood up and uttered, "Dear

gentlemen! I know this light is Holy Grail. This is the same light from which Jesus Christ drank before he proceeded to his heavenly abode. I know that this light has entered this country. I shall go after this and trace it. Unless and until I am able to trace it, I won't come back. That is my gentleman's promise."

Three other knights who were Sir Lancelot, Sir Bors and Sir Percivale uttered the same thing.

Hearing the words of the knights King Arthur felt dejected. He uttered, "For many years our Round Table has been one. But now it is broken as some of my best known knights would go after Holy Grail to find it out. Maybe I won't be able to see you again."

But the knights encouraged the King and promised that they would surely return to the palace. Out went the four knights in search of Holy Grail. They wandered every nook and corner of the country for years, but were unable to trace the Holy Grail.

After many years of wandering, all the four knights came to a place near the sea. They ascended a hill. From there, when they looked down below in the sea, they saw a ship. Although it was evening yet the ship was full of light. It was white light, more bright than sunlight. They knew that they were quite near to their destination. All of them embraced one another out of happiness. Now they descended down the hill and entered the sea. The ship had cast anchor. So, they went into the ship. It was empty. No passenger was on board. First of all, Sir Galahad went into a room. There, he saw a table upon which he saw the Holy Grail. It was shining very brightly. Afterwards all other three knights entered the room. But soon, they fell fast asleep. In the meantime, the ship again set sail for another country.

A wise old man entered the hall
and addressed the gathering.

When they opened their eyes, the ship was sailing smoothly. Soon the ship reached another city. Sir Galahad said to the other three warriors, "We had better take out this table and the Holy Grail."

Thus they took out the table and the Holy Grail, and entered the city. The King of that city was a scoundrel. Of late, he had passed away. So, the subjects of the city were divided in their opinions as to whom they should choose their new king.

In the hall, all the great and wise men were sitting. They were in discussion over the choice of their new king. A wise old man entered the hall and addressed the gathering thus, "I have chalked out a plan. In your city, four brave knights have just entered. All of them are equally courageous. But the youngest of them is the best of all. Chose him as your King. He will rule over the city in noble manners. He is sincere, truthful and valiant. He will take after his subjects with great devotion and dedication."

Saying these words the wise old man disappeared from there in an instant and was never seen again. He was the same old man who had come to the palace of King Arthur. After discussing the issue among themselves the wise men found out the youngest knight and made him their new king. So, Sir Galahad started ruling over the city from that day onwards. All the subjects were happy under his rule. As for Sir Lancelot and Sir Bors, they returned to Camelot and informed King Arthur of the proceedings. As for Sir Percival, he started living alone in the city itself. Soon, he devoted his life to God. He would sing hymns in praise of God, day in and day out.

Sir Galahad after ruling over the city for a few years

uttered one day, "I have no desire to live any longer. I have seen the divine Holy Grail. Now all my desires have been fulfilled." So, he ordered a church was constructed; he placed the Holy Grail in it.

Soon after, the same old man came to Sir Galahad and observed, "Dear son, your time on earth is finished. The mission for which you have been sent here is also complete. So go to your own abode. God calls you to Himself." Saying these words, the old man became invisible.

Next day, Sir Galahad was found dead in front of the Holy Grail. There was peace and calm on his face. All the subjects paid their last tributes to the King and buried him with stately honour.

King Arthur Breathes His Last

Sir Lancelot had grown old, so had King Arthur. Now the king had desired to renounce the throne. The time had come for the breaking up of the fellowship of the Round Table. Sir Lancelot had been searching for the Holy Grail for many years. He had travelled length and breadth of the country to trace it. But all his efforts proved an exercise in futility. Unable to trace it, he came back to Camelot sad and disappointed. His heart was broken. There in Camelot everyone was talking about his love with Queen Guinevere.

Sir Mordred was a mean knight. He always wanted to usurp the throne of Britain. He had been looking for a golden opportunity for many years. But he had not got it as yet. But now as the rumour of love between Queen Guinevere and Sir Lancelot spread though Britain, he sensed it an opportunity to carry out his nefarious design. He knew that this was the only way that he could create friction between King Arthur and his bravest warrior, Sir Lancelot. In order to cash on the rumour, he straightaway headed for King Arthur. When he met him, he told, "Sir! I have a bad news for you. There is in the air that love is sprouting between your queen and Sir Lancelot. The queen loves him and he loves her in return. It has been going on for months. The news is true to the best of my knowledge."

Hearing the news King Arthur felt shocked and

bewildered. He could not believe his ears. He had full trust in Sir Lancelot. His heart was not ready to accept that Sir Lancelot could have done this evil deed. But when Sir Mordred gave him proof, King Arthur had to believe him. Now the King flew into a rage. On the other hand, the King loved Sir Lancelot very much. He would have forgiven him had Sir Mordred along with his brother Sir Garvaine not made the King, feel very angry.

Both Sir Mordred and Sir Garvaine said to King Arthur in one voice, "Your Highness! He is a traitor. He should be banished from the country. He has brought a slur on your name. Don't pardon him in any case."

At the insistence of the two brothers King Arthur banished Sir Lancelot to France. Sir Lancelot was alone. He could not do anything as he was helpless. None came in his support. Many months passed. Sir Lancelot was living in France and passing his days peacefully there. But the two brothers were not happy still. They again came back to King Arthur and uttered, "Your Highness! Let us wage a war on Sir Lancelot. He must be killed for his nefarious deed. He has no right to live on. He is a scoundrel and has stabbed you in the back."

Thus the two brother poisoned King Arthur's ears against Sir Lancelot who was unaware of these proceedings there in Britain. At the head of a large army of soldiers King Arthur along with Sir Garvaine went to France to measure arms with Sir Lancelot. Sir Mordred remained back there in Britain to rule over the city in his absence. After King Arthur had gone, Sir Mordred got the chance he was looking for. He forged some documents as if they had come from France. Thereafter he went over to the queen and uttered, "These letters have come from France. It is stated that King Arthur died fighting against Sir Lancelot. He has appointed me the next king of Britain. So I should marry you."

Hearing the words of Sir Mordred the queen suspected some foul play. So, she acted with cleverness. She said to Sir Mordred, "I am willing to be your queen but first of all, let me go to London to buy me my new wedding gown."

Sir Mordred agreed to what the queen had said. The queen along with some trustworthy knights, left behind by King Arthur for her protection, rode to London without losing much time. Reaching there she locked herself in the tower of England. When the queen did not return even after a day or two, Sir Mordred grew suspicious. He went after the queen and found her locked in the tower of London. However hard he tried to unlock the Tower of London, all his efforts proved an exercise in futility. The walls of the tower were too strong and Sir Mordred could not break them and let himself in.

In the meantime, King Arthur came to learn of the treachery of Sir Mordred. He flew into a rage. He made a comeback instantly. With his large army he headed for Britain. Sir Mordred also gathered his army together to give a fight to King Arthur. So, he rode to Dover to fight against the King. At Dover, both Sir Mordred and King Arthur met each other. A great battle ensued between the two. Many soldiers on either side were killed. But Sir Mordred's remaining soldiers could not face the onslaught of King Arthur. So, they fled from the front. Sir Garvain, brother of Sir Mordred, was seriously wounded. He was struck with a weapon on the head. He himself knew that he was badly wounded and he had little chance of survival. Before breathing his last he said to King Arthur, "O King! I am near the death-bed. Give me a pen and paper so that I may write to Sir Lancelot."

After the King had handed the pen and paper over to him, he wrote to Sir Lancelot as follows :

"Sir! It is a very crucial time. Come here quickly to protect King Arthur as his life is in danger. I beg your pardon from the bottom of my heart for poisoning the king's ears against you. Be here at once and save your king."

After writing this much he died.

King Arthur gave the letter to one of his men and ordered him to deliver it to Sir Lancelot. In the meantime, Sir Mordred had gathered more men to attack the King. Next morning at the head of a large army Sir Mordred marched towards the king to measure arms with him. King Arthur was staying near the lake, where he along with Merlin had gone to get Excalibur, the wonderful sword. The night before the final battle King Arthur saw Sir Garvaine in his dream. Sir Garvaine said to the King, "Sire! Don't fight against Sir Mordred. He is stronger than you. Wait till Sir Lancelot along with his army reaches here."

Next day as King Arthur awoke, his dream had disappeared. He called all his remaining knights and said, "There will be no fighting from today onwards. You have to keep your swords in their scabbards. If any of the soldiers of Sir Mordred takes out of his sword from the scabbard only then you will kill him. Come along with me."

There in the camp of Sir Mordred a messenger came and delivered the message thus, "Sire! King Arthur is coming to have a discussion with you. If any of your soldiers takes out his sword from the scabbard only then his soldiers will fight and kill the soldier."

On the stipulated time, King Arthur along with his army of soldiers met Sir Mordred. He was very alert and active. On the other hand, Sir Mordred was equally agile. None of the soldiers on either side took out their swords from their scabbards. Everything went smoothly. King Arthur had a peaceful discussion with Sir Mordred.

All the soldiers of both Sir Mordred and King Arthur were standing silently. All of a sudden, a snake crawled out of the grass and bit a knight on his foot. The knight took out his sword and killed the snake there and then. No sooner did the knight put his hand to the sword than all the knights on either side took out their swords from the scabbards. Soon they began to fight among themselves. There ensued a fierce battle between Sir Mordred and King Arthur. The fight continued till evening. On King Arthur's side, only two knights—Sir Lucan and Sir Bedivere were alive. All other knights had been brutally killed at the hands of the soldiers of Sir Mordred. On Sir Mordred's side his all soldiers had been put to death. He stood alone with his sword. Out of Sir Lucan and Sir Bedivere, the former was badly wounded. He needed immediate treatment.

Seeing so much bloodshed King Arthur flew into a rage. He ran wildly at Sir Mordred with a spear in his right hand. The spear went through the body of Sir Mordred who fell down lifeless there and then. Before breathing his last, he was able to wound King Arthur seriously. Seeing the pitiable condition of their King Sir Lucan and Sir Bedivere took the King to a nearby church which stood near the field. They set the King down. In the meantime, Sir Lucan succumbed to his wounds. Now Sir Bedivere was left alone to take care of King Arthur.

Seeing Sir Bedivere in front of him King Arthur said to him, "O dear! My death is approaching. Now I am not going to live any more. Take this sword of mine and throw it into the lake."

Thus King Arthur handed over his Excalibur to Sir Bedivere who readily accepted to do what the King had asked him to do. He ran through the forest to the lakeside. After reaching there, as he was about to throw it into the water, the jewels in the hilt flashed and shone.

Sir Bedivere thought, 'It is such a beautiful sword. It is no use throwing it into the water. It is expensive as well. I shall keep if for my use.' Thinking so he hid the sword there in the field and came back to King Arthur. When King Arthur asked him whether he had thrown the sword into the lake or not, he replied that he had thrown it. When the King asked him what he saw there, he replied that he had seen the water, the sky, the stone and the grass.

Thereupon King Arthur chided him saying, "You are telling a lie. It means you have not thrown it into the lake." Sir Bedivere again went to the lake and came back pretending that he had thrown it. But when the King asked him what he had seen, he replied that he had seen the water, the stones, the sky and the grass.

This time again, King Arthur saw through his trick and scolded him severely thus, "This is the last chance you have. Either throw the sword into the water or get killed."

Now Sir Bedivere took the sword out of its hiding place and threw it into the lake with all his might. Hardly had he thrown the sword into the water when an arm came up out of the water and caught the sword. The arm took the sword down into the lake for good. From that day onwards, the Excalibur, the wonderful sword was never seen again.

Sir Bedivere came back to the King and told him

what he had seen. Now the King was confirmed that Sir Bedivere had really thrown the sword into the water. King Arthur said to Sir Bedivere, "Dear, please take me to the lake."

When they reached the lake, the King saw a black barge at the side of the lake. There, beautiful queens dressed in black were sitting. After looking at the faces of the queens the King thought that they were the queens whom he had known and who had died. He longed to be with the queens. Sir Bedivere set the King down on the barge. The queens stood around the King. In a trice, the King breathed his last and the queen buried him there and then. But King Arthur's grave was never found there. Thus ended the golden era of truthfulness, chivalry, bravery with the passing away of King Arthur.

After the death of King Arthur, Sir Lancelot came to Camelot. When he learnt of the passing away of the King, he plunged into an ocean of grief and sadness. He wept bitterly.

Now, he had nobody to support him. Some of the knights of King Arthur had been killed in the fight, whereas some others had left for their respective kingdoms. The fellowship of the Round Table had broken up with the death of King Arthur who built a very large empire and united all the powerful knights from different walks of life under the same roof. Sir Lancelot too did not live long. After a few months he passed away in his sleep. He was buried near a church with stately honour.

As for Queen Guinevere, she was distraught and overwhelmed with grief. She gave up the throne and joined a nunnery. There, she spent rest of her life devoted to prayer and noble deeds. ❐

Questions Based on the Story

Chapter-1
Arthur is Crowned King

Q. 1 Whose son was Arthur, the Great?

Q. 2 Who was Merlin? What did he ask King Arthur to do?

Chapter-2
The Fellowship of Knights

Q. 1 Who defeated the Saxon pirates and how?

Q. 2 What was the fellowship of the knights of the Round Table?

Chapter-3
Arthur Befriends Sir Pellinore

Q. 1 How did Arthur come by the wonderful sword, Excalibur?"

Q. 2 What does Excalibur mean?

Chapter-4
Arthur's Scabbard is Lost

Q. 1 Who stole the scabbard of King Arthur and why?

Q. 2 Who was Morgan le Fay?

Chapter-5
Arthur Welcomes Lancelot

Q. 1 Who was Sir Lancelot? To which country did he belong?

Q. 2 Why did Merlin feel sad when Queen Guinevere and Sir Lancelot exchanged glances with each other?

Chapter-6
Gareth Marries Linet

Q. 1 What were the three gifts of Gareth?

Q. 2 What were the names of the four knights who took away the sister of lady Linet?

Chapter-7
Geraint Wins the Golden Falcon

Q. 1 Who was presented with the Golden Falcon?

Q. 2 What did Geraint say when Enid's father told that Enid had no beautiful clothes?

Chapter-8
Breunor Saves the Queen

Q. 1 What did Breunor tell King Arthur about his wearing on old torn coat?

Q. 2 How did Breunor manage to earn a position in the Fellowship of the Knights of the Round Table?

Chapter–9
Sir Meligrance is Killed

Q. 1 What condition did Queen Guinevere put before
Sir Melligrance before being taken away by him
to his palace?

Q. 2 How did Sir Lancelot manage to escape from the
dungeon?

Chapter–10
Holy Grail

Q. 1 What did the old man dressed in white and with
a white beard say to King Arthur?

Q. 2 What was the Holy Grail? Who put it inside the
church?

Chapter–11
King Arthur Breathes His Last

Q. 1 Who poisoned King Arthur's ears against Sir
Lancelot and why?

Q. 2 How did King Arthur meet with his end?